PRAISE FOR
TEENFLUENCER NATION

Kiera Colson is an ambitious and talented entrepreneur and author. Wise beyond her years, Kiera fearlessly pursues her life passions and goals both personally and professionally with laser focus. Don't take your eyes off this young woman; she is destined for success.

—Kasey Trenum, Crazy Hot Mess Express Out of Control Homeschooling Blogger Who Makes Yummy Chicken and Veggies

I have had the honor of seeing first-hand the powerful and life-changing impact Kiera is having on teens from around the country. From the big stage to small groups to one-on-one, Kiera has been gifted with the passion and insight to lead her generation to real and meaningful change for the future. *Teenfluencer Nation* is an entertaining, thought-provoking, and practical book that inspires real-life action to live your best life possible. How do I know? Because Kiera's inspired me to do just that. I highly recommend *Teenfluencer Nation* for teens and for those of us who have outgrown our teen years too.

—Doug Fitzgerald, Best-Selling Author and Host of *OneShot. OneLife.* Podcast

Author and speaker Kiera Colson writes from the heart. Her first book *Twin Tales* explored mystically faith-based stories under the sea. *Teenfluencer Nation* is an example of faith over fear and how God is working in every part of our lives if you just listen. She has shared in detail how she took her anxiety and anger and transformed that energy to create and connect. I have the pleasure of knowing Kiera and her family personally and she has been blessed to carry the message of hope during the hard times of adolescence. It has been amazing to watch her morph into a teen boss and provide a platform for other teens to share their stories and connect.

—Crystal Waltman, CrystalWaltman.com,
Author of *Quitting to Win: A Proven Plan to Let Go of Bad Habits, Learn to Feel, and Love Yourself*,
Athlete, Speaker, and Coach

TEENFLUENCER NATION

Also by Kiera Colson

Twin Tales
Twin Tales Coloring Book

TEENFLUENCER NATION

Teens Standing Out In A World Pressing In

a Movement by Teens for Teens

KIERA COLSON

Teenfluencer Nation ©2022 by Kiera Colson.

All rights reserved. Printed in the USA.

Published by Author Academy Elite
P.O. Box 43, Powell, OH 43065
www.AuthorAcademyElite.com

All rights reserved. No part of this publication may be reproduced, stored in a retrieval system, or transmitted in any form or by any means—for example, electronic, photocopy, recording—without the prior written permission of the publisher. The only exception is brief quotations in printed reviews.

Library of Congress Cataloging

Paperback: 978-1-946114-99-0
Hardcover: 979-8-88583-035-5
E-book: 979-8-88583-104-8

Available in hardback, softcover, and e-book.

To protect the privacy of those who have shared their stories with the author, some details and names have been changed. Any internet addresses (websites, blogs, etc.) and telephone numbers printed in this book are offered as a resource. They are not intended in any way to be or imply an endorsement by Author Academy Elite, nor does Author Academy Elite vouch for the content of these sites and numbers for the life of this book.

DEDICATION

For all the teens with a story, a dream, and a passion uniquely their own.

Hint: That's you.

To Morgo. To Caleb. To Michael. To Dallas. To Ari. To Jonathan. To Grace. To Zyla-Ray. To Bontle. To Lisa. To Kary. To the Trenums. To Coach Golden. To my family. To all the relationships that have impacted who I am becoming.

Thank you. None of this would be possible without you because this is all for you.

TABLE OF CONTENTS

Praise for Teenfluencer Nation i
Dedication vii
Foreword. xiii
Note to the Reader xv
Introduction xvii

PART 1
TEN CHALLENGES THAT TEENS FACE

Challenge One: Tormented Nights and Traumatic Days (Change). 3
Challenge Two: Alone in a School Full of People (Relationships) 7
Challenge Three: Obsessed with My Image (Identity). . 15
Challenge Four: Failing to Make the Grade (Disappointment) 22
Challenge Five: Pushing through the Pain (Goals) 27
Challenge Six: Underneath the Smile (Authenticity). . . 33
Challenge Seven: Unanswered Questions (Faith). 37
Challenge Eight: Bigger Than Me (Service) 43
Challenge Nine: Part of the Solution (Participation) . . . 46
Challenge Ten: Around the Corner (Uncertainty) 53

PART 2
12 CHARACTERISTICS THAT TEENS NEED

Characteristic One: Impact 65
Characteristic Two: Belonging 73
Characteristic Three: Confidence 77
Characteristic Four: Standards 82
Characteristic Five: Focus 87
Characteristic Six: Value 92
    Friendships 92
    Boyfriend/Girlfriend 97
    Siblings 102
    Parents 106
Characteristic Seven: Wisdom 109
Characteristic Eight: Patience 114
Characteristic Nine: Adaptability 119
Characteristic Ten: Connection 124
Characteristic Eleven: Enjoyment 127
Characteristic Twelve: Reflection 132

PART 3
10 CASE STUDIES: WHAT TEENS CAN BECOME

Case Study One: Rachel Scott
    (August 5, 1981–April 20, 1999) 145
Case Study Two: Queen Esther Hadassa of Persia
    (400–500 BC) 147
Case Study Three: Louis Braille
    (January 4, 1809–January 6, 1852) 150

Case Study Four: Mary Lou Retton
    (January 24, 1968 –Present)................. 151
Case Study Five: Michael Phelps
    (June 30, 1985–Present)..................... 152
Case Study Six: Dwight Gooden
    (November 16, 1964 –Present)................ 154
Case Study Seven: Michael Jackson
    (August 29, 1958–June 25, 2009).............. 156
Case Study Eight: King David of Israel & Judah
    (1035–970 BC)............................. 158
Case Study Nine: Anne Frank
    (June 12, 1929–February/March 1945)......... 160
Case Study Ten: You (Right Now!) 162

A Special Invitation from the Author 163
About the Author 165

FOREWORD

Teens often get the impression they don't matter. They're caught in the "in between."

In between child and adult.

In between immaturity and responsibility.

In between restrictions and privilege.

Nevertheless, teenagers do matter. They're a major focus of marketers, retailers, and movie makers. By using sophisticated efforts and big money, such people seek to influence teens and their purchasing decisions.

I see this struggle in my three teenagers. They see it with their friends.

Stepping back for a moment, one realizes that teenagers, though young, though seemingly insignificant, are the focus of powerful marketing companies, advertising agencies, Hollywood moguls, and global influencers. This reflects their importance within culture and society.

The truth is teens matter much more than as a segment of consumers.

Teenfluencer Nation captures this belief. Author Kiera Colson, a teen herself, exhorts teenagers to refrain from merely being influenced. She invites them to become Teenfluencers. Kiera's transparency and raw style connects with her contemporaries. She reminds them they were created for greatness.

Adults who read this book will get an inside look into the mind of teen unwilling to get her daily marching orders from big corporations or powerful media agencies.

Teenfluencer Nation is a tool that awakens a youthful army to rise up and leverage their passions, energies, and gifts to positively impact the world. Teens shouldn't be bought. They should be invested in. They're not merely pawns in a money-making metaverse. Teenagers are capable of making significant contributions to the world.

Both teens and adults alike will see the challenges, characteristics, and case studies confronting young people. A word of warning. If you read this book with an open heart, get ready to join the movement.

—Kary Oberbrunner,
Wall Street Journal and *USA Today* best-selling author, and CEO of Igniting Souls Publishing Agency

NOTE TO THE READER

As a teen conquering high school, I am sure you are incredibly busy. You might just want the facts. I will honor your request by showing you to Part 2 where you will skip my story and learn the characteristics of a Teenfluencer.

A quick word of warning, however.

If you skip Part 1, time will be saved, but you will miss out on the transformation. The reason being is in Part 1, I share things I have never shared to anyone else before—my flaws!

I could have turned away from sharing these imperfections, but then I would fail to reach my goal—being authentic with you. I believe my heartache, confusion, determination, and story development from my past will give you a greater hope for your future.

If I can become a Teenfluencer, then I have no doubt that you can too.

Whether you start with Part 1 or Part 2, I can't wait to join you on your journey to becoming a part of Teenfluencer Nation.

Are you ready?

Let's begin.

—Kiera Colson

INTRODUCTION

A young middle-school girl walks past her dreaded floor-length mirror. She glances at herself—wild blond hair, smeared makeup, and tired eyes. A sigh fills the room as her body steps over yesterday's laundry and sinks into her poorly-made bed. Head hitting her pillow, her eyelids slowly close. Yet that is merely the signal for her brain to kick in.

Ideas, visions, and thoughts bounce around in the girl's head, trying to claim her attention. Twisting and turning, anxiety begins to fill her stomach. The "what ifs" and "should haves" of life start to declare victory over her thoughts. Scenarios of the day flash before her eyes.

All her mistakes threaten to consume her. The so-called truths echo in her brain. She tries shutting her eyes harder.

Why can't I just force myself to sleep?
I don't want to think.
I just want to sleep.

The "to dos" of tomorrow flood her brain:

- *Test in science on the cells.*
- *Christiana needs help editing her essay.*
- *Suicides at basketball practice.*

The reminders that the girl is alone and the future paths to embarrassment consume her. A heavy weight presses on her heart. It's now hard to think as tears begin building up inside her. Darkness is all she can see, eyes open or closed.

A pain strikes her side as she thinks of her past: *regret*.
Tears escape her eyes as she thinks of her present: *disgust*.
Does she think of her future? *No.*

Those thoughts were unmarked and unclear. Her mind alone knew what was and what is. Not what could be. *Would she find a way to survive?*

Only time would tell.

PART 1

TEN CHALLENGES THAT TEENS FACE

CHALLENGE ONE

TORMENTED NIGHTS AND TRAUMATIC DAYS (CHANGE)

When we are no longer able to change a situation, we are challenged to change ourselves.

—Viktor E. Frankl

For years, this was my reality, night after night.

At times, I was my own worst enemy trapped inside my own mind. I dreaded the period of time spent lying in bed before drifting off to sleep. My brain did not know how to stop. I had so much hate targeted at myself.

I hated my home. I hated my life.

Being alone with thoughts driven by such hate is terrifying and never leads to anything good.

These nights began to happen when I was awakened from my childhood fantasy. The fantasy where I was the most popular and boy-adored girl in my elementary school. It was a small school, so since kindergarten I had had my best friends in all my classes. Learning was fun and, of course, there were the daily adventures. Such as "swimming" through the halls, sneaking over to the "big" kids' territory, an intense game of tag at recess, or the epic kickball games in gym class.

At this time, I lived in Tennessee with my grandmother, who I call Nana; she was always cooking something delicious. My day would consist of waking up to breakfast with a view of the Great Smoky Mountains, playing fairytale games on the four acres that my siblings and I claimed as our playground, and learning the sounds of music from the very heart of our home.

Sixth grade came and went, and I didn't give it another thought. Life was simple. Eat. Play. Learn. Sleep. Repeat.

Until one day, everything changed.

• • •

"Colson Crew, come in the den. Family meeting." A mother's and father's hearts break as they sit down on the large gray couch. The harmony of tiny footsteps fills the room as the summoned children come pounding from all directions.

As the oldest child, I charge in with a competitive heart, determined to be first to the den. My mind wanders as my hair tosses through the air.

Were we getting a puppy?

Or maybe we were going to play Mario Kart?

Blasting past my parents, I fling myself onto the couch in triumph, "I win!" My younger siblings pile onto the couch seconds behind me.

"We weren't racing, Kiera. No one even said "start." Makena, the second born, huffs. "First is the worst, second is the best, anyways!" The usual sibling rivalry.

"So, are we going to Disney?" Aliyah, my youngest sister, screams at the top of her lungs.

"Hey, I was gonna guess that," Tegan, the baby boy, smirks. "But if she's wrong, I wasn't gonna say that." Laughter burst from all four of us innocent children.

With a shifting of position, my father clears his throat. Silence arises. All of us instantly can sense the atmospheric change. Whatever our father was about to say was serious. I just knew something was wrong. Searching my brain, confusion filled my mind.

Did I do something?

Did I leave all my toys out?

Did I say something mean to Aliyah?

I couldn't remember anything.

Then my father began to speak in his pastor language, "This has been such a great season in your life. God has blessed you by helping you make so many friends and create great experiences. But sometimes seasons change."

Now, at this point, the amount of confusion crashing around in my brain was overwhelming. *What in the world did seasons have to do with any of this?*

"We love you guys so much." The sound of my mother's voice rang out through the air. "We wouldn't ever do anything that we did not think was the best for you. God has been so great to us. Now, sometimes God sends people on adventures and can even send families like ours on missions."

Working in overtime, my mind at this point is barely comprehending what they are saying. Glancing to the right, I notice my Nana walk into the room. Tears streamed down her face at an alarming rate. The sound of her blowing her nose rends the rare quiet. Devastation is painted across her face.

If my mom was talking about adventure, then why was my Nana so sad?

"Look us in the eye," my mother's soothing voice commanded. All of us children instantly looked up, watching as she let out a deep breath, glancing at my father. He nodded, and our mother put on a fake smile, her eyes watering, and with a forced excitement. "We are moving to South Carolina!"

Instantly, utter shock swept through my body. I could not breathe. Emotional pain fueled my veins as tears started rushing down my face.

"I don't want to go. I *won't* go," I exclaimed. The feeling of my world crumbling down before me threatened to drag me down with it. I knew of no other life.

I did not want to leave my home.

My friends.

My Nana.

I do not understand.

Shock slowly turned to anger as my body erupted from the den, and I thrust myself toward my bedroom.

• • •

There is a moment in time when we start to leave behind our childhood perspectives. We begin to enter a time of trial and error, a place where we unknowingly trust misconceptions and false realities. We learn the truth about the likes of people and the ways of the world.

My fairytale childhood started its last chapter during my sixth-grade year with no fairytale ending. In fact, it ended so abruptly that there are days when I wish to escape back to the time before that book closed, the time that existed before I knew what anxiety, betrayal, hurt, perfectionism, and disappointment were. Before I started a new chapter called adolescence.

CHALLENGE TWO

ALONE IN A SCHOOL FULL OF PEOPLE (RELATIONSHIPS)

> Oh yes, the past can hurt. But the way I see it, you can either run from it or learn from it.
>
> —Rafiki (*The Lion King*)

The cold glass of the van window chilled my face as I longingly stared out at the passing greenery. The song "Remember Me" from the Disney Channel TV Show *Shake It Up*, filled my ears.

Anger fueled through my veins as I watched myself ride further and further from the life I once had. Tears threatened to fall once more. With each ride to and from Tennessee and South Carolina, I continued to find myself left alone with my thoughts with no one to share them.

• • •

For five months, my family traveled to and from Tennessee and South Carolina every Friday and Sunday.

For five months, I kept "Remember Me" on replay.

As I have grown, I have realized that the music I listen to connects to the season of life I am going through. There are times when I can't explain how I am feeling but I can find a song whose lyrics ring true to my heart. It all seems to connect.

"Remember Me" was the very first song I truly connected to and that helped me express how I was feeling and the first song that made me cry, and to this day, sends me back to that little girl staring out that blue van window.

> *"I wish that we could do it over again,*
> *Every smile, every tear, every part . . .*
> *Whatever will be, I'll remember you so remember me."*
> — "Remember Me," from *Shake It Up* by Zendaya

When I rode the lonesome mountain roads between South Carolina and Tennessee, I was consumed with the fear that my friends would forget about me.

During sleepovers, my friends and classmates would pull out their old yearbooks, and I would become *that* girl. *That* girl people see in their yearbooks but never remember.

I feared being forgotten.

To this day, I get a heavy feeling when I think of those lyrics because it sends me down a road of what could have been. It reminds me of all the graduations, basketball games, dances, and plans that I missed out on because I was hours away living in another state.

• • •

At the time when we found out we were moving, I was still in school. My parents were doing their best to make the move as easy as possible but, in reality, it was hard. The church my parents had been leading for fourteen years was swept from beneath their feet due to the lies and wickedness of spurious people within the church.

About this time, I had begun growing bitter toward the church because I felt I could not trust those associated with church. Parents would influence their kids to be friends with me so they could get to my parents. People who my parents had been pouring their lives into took everything and never looked back.

My parents had to move on or they would have been stuck in a poverty mindset for another decade.

(At the time, my siblings and I were too young to comprehend the hardship that this church was putting on my parents.)

When you look back at your childhood, can you remember when your innocent mindset changed?

When life was no longer all about just enjoying the simple things?

Sometimes I really wish I could go back to being unaware of the cruelty of the world.

• • •

Our process in moving to South Carolina was adventurous for sure. For instance:

- We stayed in hotels and other church members' houses as we searched for our new home.
- My mom's arm was crushed during the move by the moving truck's door.
- My mom got bit by a rat. *Seriously*, she did.
- We had to do our laundry at our new church for months.
- The entire first floor of our new home flooded the second day after we moved in (causing us to move back out two weeks before school started).

- My mom was across the world when my dad bought our house. (She literally Facetimed my dad when we were looking at our house for the first time.)
- My mom had two things she wanted in her new house: a place for her sixteen-foot Disney Christmas tree and white cabinets. She got neither, but we managed to attach our tree to the side of the stairs, perfectly positioning the top of the tree in the open stairwell.

Moving from four acres to having neighbors ten feet away was shocking. But, changing from a school with eighty people in your grade to four hundred people was total culture shock.

• • •

My eyes grew wide as we pulled up to this gigantic, glass-detailed, three-story building. My entire family looked like a deer in headlights. Our eyes continued to grow wider as we went over the fact that this was not just a school, but a public middle school.

It looked like an airport!

The glass windows shimmered, and the gator green decor let off a professionalism unlike any that I had ever seen before. Piling out of the blue van, my family of six slowly made our way up the long side that led to the heart of the Gators.

A fresh breeze hit our faces as we swung open the door to the front office. Kids were buzzing in and out like bees heading to classes, reuniting with old friends, a controlled chaos.

"Good luck today," my mom whispered. My hand shook as I grasped my Tennessee Volunteer-themed lunchbox.

Would I make new friends?

Would I have nice teachers?

I turned to start my seventh grade adventure at my new school. Heart racing, I stepped into the main hall of the school to face a crowd of students in the gigantic cafeteria. I searched for a seat somewhere past the cafe booths and lunch tables.

Wait?

Why is there a stage in the cafeteria?

That's a *bit* much.

My eyes identified an empty seat in a booth to the far right. Carefully, I made my way past the screaming middle school girls and taunting guys. My legs trembled as I sat down. My fingertips traced the seams of my lunchbox making up the "Power T."

For the first time in my life, I sat alone.

Alone in a building full of thousands of people.

• • •

Being alone is a terrifying feeling, and many teens and adults dread it. There is nothing scarier than going through the trials of life having no one to turn to. When we were younger and a nightmare would cause us to fear, we would crawl out of bed calling our mom's name.

• • •

Pushing through the door to your parent's room, your shaking body shuffles toward the dark silhouette of your mother. Startled, your mother shoots up out of bed as you poke her awake.

"Huh?" Panic quickly rises in her voice, "What's wrong?"

You cry out, "I had a bad dream. Can I sleep with you?"

She sighs. "Of course." Your body relaxes as the warmth of your parents' bed calls you back into a deep sleep.

• • •

As we get older, the idea of being alone in the depths of night transforms into being alone in life. One of the greatest struggles is when you're in a season of life where you feel like you're gonna fall and you turn around but no one is there. It's scary how easily people you know can become people you don't know.

• • •

When I was in seventh grade, I got sucked into a couple of friendships that would later reveal themselves as toxic. These new "friends" were the ones who were talking behind my back, using me for my grades, my kindness, and even the loyalty of my friendship.

For me, every time a friend betrayed a relationship, I would blame myself. If they did not want to be my friend, then I thought something must be wrong with me.

The only problem was that these girls had a different definition of friendship. When I chose to be friends with someone, I was going to be there for them no matter what. The reality is that most relationships are temporary, but all relationships have the potential to leave a lasting impact.

I know what it's like to have friends change into bullies. Girls who mock and use you, especially in high school, can tear down your confidence as fast as wildfires spread.

Freshman year of high school, I let my personality hide away in a shell. I was quiet and careful to speak because of the girls who were speaking negatively about me. I hated who I was, partly due to them.

It was time to make a decision.

Would I be the one who stands alone in the crowd, or would I be the one who stands alone on the winner's podium?

Every day during freshman year, I found myself sitting at a table with girls who were messing around with boys in the most impure ways. They were gossiping, fighting about politics, and tearing each other down over grades and athletic performances.

I hated sitting there, unsure what to say when I had no interest in contributing to their conversations nor participating in their actions. It took courage and time, but one day I decided I did not need to be friends with them anymore.

They had controlled me through middle school and into high school. It was time that I let go of the leash they had attached to me.

• • •

Heart racing, I turned right instead of left. The tiny voice in my head screamed.

What if they see us?

What if they ask where I am?

Walking up to the highest point of the courtyard, I let out a sigh of relief as I rested my school bag on the white circular table. Glancing out across the green grass toward the glass doors leading to the cafeteria, I watched as my "friends" made their way inside.

Turning my head away, I noticed some aspiring dancers and musicians expressing their passions upon the low brick walls that framed the courtyard. They danced and played without fear. I wanted that type of confidence and assurance in what I was doing. A cool breeze tossed my hair into the wind as I reached for my Bible.

Today, I had made a choice to be alone in the physical but not in the spiritual sense.

• • •

Looking back, it's scary how much I allowed others to control me. It only takes one repetitive action to break a chain that is holding you down. For me, it was not sitting with the girls who were bullying me day after day.

Sometimes it only takes one small step or action to take you into your next.

After that day, I would be tempted.

Would I stand around in FCA (Fellow Christian Athletes) Club during worship, or would I dance, fully expressing my worship?

Would I discard my parents' advice and protest a movement with my friends, or would I stand alone in an empty classroom praying for my friends' protection instead?

Would I choose to be lazy and disrespectful like the rest of my basketball team, or would I push thr*ough the pain and not stop until the buzzer sounds?*

Every day you make choices and decisions that have the ability to shape who you will become in the future.

I am not going to lie and say it's going to be easy.

It's not.

In fact, it's easier to follow the crowd. But if you want to do extraordinary things, then you are going to have to step out of your comfort zone and believe you can do the impossible.

Trust me, there will be a time in your life when you will need to stand alone. Make sure when it comes, you are ready.

CHALLENGE THREE

OBSESSED WITH MY IMAGE (IDENTITY)

> **Why worry? If you've done the very best you can, worrying won't make it any better.**
>
> —Walt Disney

My body ached. My heart pounded as I screamed out in the night. Mind racing, worries consumed every bit of my being. This fight to stop my thoughts from beating away at me continued every night from seventh to tenth Grade.

I was angry at God.
I was angry at the church.
I was angry at my parents.
I was frustrated that I did not have the friendship connection that I was craving.

School was beginning to consume me, and I hated myself. I was so extremely stressed over getting 100s that I would fall to the ground and weep when I did not achieve those goals. I could not process all the thoughts of failure rushing through my mind.

• • •

No one ever saw this side of me, except my parents. Outside the walls of my home, I was always smiling, and I seemed to have it all together.

Yet within, I was plagued with thoughts such as

- *Suck in your tummy.*
- *You look thick.*
- *You look like a stick.*

My mind was overwhelmed as I went from middle school to high school.

These sayings echoed within me every time I passed a mirror. The perfected images of the girls I saw on TV and social media bullied my mind every time I saw a picture of myself. I could not understand how all the girls looked so perfect, so beautiful, so unlike me.

And I hated it. I hated *me* because of it.

This caused me to lose all confidence in the way I looked. My body image perspectives were skewed.

Then the false information that food companies marketed started to fill my mind. I began to eat less and work out more. I got to the point that I was eating only nine hundred calories a day and then binging over the weekend.

I was obsessed.

Every time I looked in the mirror, I wanted to cry. If someone even brought up going shopping for clothes, I dreaded every moment leading up to it. I was seconds from bursting into tears wherever I was. I would read these diet guides and rules that so-called "experts" claimed to be true and take them as facts. For instance, I read that it was best not to eat after seven pm.

So, what did I do?

After not eating breakfast and half a slice of pita bread for lunch, I would be so hungry that I would binge eat around six pm. I vividly remember night after night watching the clock turn to seven and I would put my fork down and would not eat any more. Even if I was hungry.

I thought it was how you were supposed to feel. That feeling where all your senses are working on overdrive, and you can't think about anything but food. I thought every girl just had to do this to be beautiful. Little did I know that most of the models and actresses I looked up to were getting nose jobs and using filters.

This is a condition that teen girls deal with that I call "airbrush anxiety."

When you are younger, it's hard to tell truth from lies. At some point, the false truths that were being spoken to me and displayed before me started to become my truth. I was comparing my perfectly imperfect body to a "perfected" body. I slowly began to despise the idea of food. It didn't happen overnight, but it was a hole that I was slowly digging myself into.

No one noticed, and if they did, I had no interest in listening to them.

To this day, I can fall into the trap. I swipe through Instagram, wishing I could look like her. Only to realize the girl I was looking at has changed her appearance with a filter, Photoshop, Botox, or implants. The list of ways to change one's imagination is endless. Heaven forbid the number of times I have been looking at a man thinking it's a woman and comparing myself to the image.

As I gathered input from my friends on what they struggled with as a teen, the number one thing for the girls was having trouble loving themselves in their own skin. It makes my blood boil because even as I write this book, I am struggling with it. It's hard.

I have to be honest that even though I have come a long way, I still compare. I don't even know if it is possible not to compare. But we do have the power to not let comparison control us.

• • •

For about two to three years, I was in a bad place when it came to my body image.

I barely ate.

I was angry all the time, and I was weak.

Plus, I was anxious, mentally tired, and completely stripped from my identity.

Fun was a distant memory.

During this time, I only focused on school, my body, and the past. It was a dark hole that haunted me every day. It felt like I had no one to turn to. I had no idea that other people were struggling with the same things.

We all have these regrets, things that impact us that can either make us stronger or that have the power to control us.

For me, when I had fallen into this self-dug hole, I would cry myself to sleep every night, thinking about what could have been or who I should be. I was the most critical perfectionist when it came to myself. If I felt like I was not perfect or if I did not do something perfectly, I saw myself as a failure.

The hard part, if you know a perfectionist or are one, is that we tend to think we are right or our way is right. We don't like getting help from other people because we end up fixing it anyways. No one could tell me that what I was doing to myself was bad. I had to learn it for myself, and it all happened in one moment.

A moment when I realized everything needed to change, or I'd end up losing my life.

∙ ∙ ∙

It was exam week, and I had been so nervous that I hadn't eaten in two days. My heart pounded in my chest as I laid down to sleep.

Around midnight, I woke up barely breathing, gasping for breath because my body was so low on nutrients and my hormones were irregular. I had to force myself to eat. That night I could have been hospitalized from malnutrition.

All of this happened because I allowed myself to believe in the "truths" of the world.

The "truth" that you must look a certain way or act a certain way to be loved. As a result, I was hurting my body in a way that wasn't allowing it to function properly. After that night, I made a decision that I would never forcibly go without food again.

In my mind, I was beginning to realize that food fuels our bodies, just as gas fuels a car. I promised myself that I would educate myself correctly in nutrition and fitness. I am grateful for that experience because without it, I never would have gained an appreciation for weightlifting or food itself.

Did it take time to return to a healthier way of living?

Yes, it took me about three years of trial and error until I fell in love with weightlifting and cooking whole foods.

And am I finished with the journey?

No way! Now I eat all the time and love to cook. (Not that I cook the most delicious things. Sometimes when you try to make something "healthy," it does not turn out great.)

We have a choice either to wake up and be disappointed in how we look or feel, or we can stand up and enjoy the day that we are given.

∙ ∙ ∙

Life is made up of lessons that take some of us longer to learn because we have to reach a breaking point first to see where we need fixing. I understand now that we all have unique body types and needs, just as we have unique purposes and personalities.

Even today, it can be hard when I look in the mirror and see only the ugly.

For a second, I'll think, *Well, if I lost five pounds, then I would look so much better.* There are times when I look at myself in pictures and wonder why my cheeks are so chubby. But like I was saying before, our bodies are always changing. I can wake up and have nicely defined abs, but by the end of the day, it looks like I ate an entire watermelon.

Does a part of me still want abs 24/7? Of course; who wouldn't?

But I know it's not the most important thing in my life. Plus, it's just not realistic. Life is about balance. Of course, I think I will always still want to improve my strength and way of eating because knowledge, our bodies, and we are everchanging.

I have learned to do it in a healthier, more balanced way. And to tell you the truth, being strong and powerful is way better than forcing yourself to be skinny.

If you look in the mirror and you don't see the beauty of who you are, then I am going to share with you a trick that I did to help myself break free from my false reality.

All over my room, on my mirrors, the walls, my laptop, etc., I began to write words of affirmation that reminded me of who I really am. I would write "Beautiful" on a sticky note and place it on my laptop, "Joyful" would be signed in an Expo® marker across my mirror, and "Confident" would read on my door. I placed affirming positive words everywhere so that no matter where I looked, I was reminded of the person I am and wanted to become.

How about you? Do you need a reminder of who you are? Are you at a breaking point?

If you are, remember, we all will face breaking points that may leave scars. You will stay where you are unless you decide to change. It's a mentality game.

CHALLENGE FOUR

FAILING TO MAKE THE GRADE (DISAPPOINTMENT)

> **Just because it's what's done, doesn't mean it's what should be done.**
> —Cinderella (*Cinderella*)

When you think of the word "grade," what comes to mind?

The number and letter at the top of your test?

The thing that says whether you passed your class or not? The year of school you are in?

According to Google, the word "grade" has two different meanings.

1. a particular level of rank, quality, proficiency, intensity, or value.
2. a mark indicating the quality of a student's work.

As I went from one grade level to the next, I started falling victim to a perfectionist mentality. I thought I needed to achieve straight A's and be the overachiever in everything to be accepted.

Where did I get this from?

Perhaps from my competitive spirit?
Or my want to succeed?
Or had I developed an unhealthy amount of pride?

The first time I ever recall stressing over a grade was in first grade on a spelling *pre*test.

• • •

Jumping into the blue van my mom always drove, my backpack thudded against the backseat as my empty lunch bag landed across the seats.

"How was your day?" my mom inquired as I buckled my seat belt, followed by my three younger siblings.

"Today has been pretty good. My friends and I played *Shake It Up* on the playground, and I was Rocky." Words escaped my mouth as I started rummaging through my backpack to pull out the spelling test I had taken that morning.

Every Thursday, we had a pretest. If we made a 100 on Thursday, we did not have to take the spelling test on Friday. I had never taken the test on Friday.

As I grabbed my paper, a gasp left me.

For the first time in my entire life, I did not see the drawn 100 with the two eyes and a mouth smiling right back at me.

No.

I faced a 95 with a *WOW* sticker. I did *not* want to see a *WOW* sticker. The flood gates broke as I tossed the paper aside in the most dramatic way and screamed.

• • •

Now, you may find this quite funny. And I do now, but back then and until tenth grade, I found my entire value in my grades. For me, seventh grade is when it really started to become an obsession. I would stay up till three am every night working on projects and homework.

Everything I did, I gave 120 percent effort.

I would lose all mental capacity if I messed up. I would sit in utmost shock because of the fact that I had failed. My parents told me to do my best, but they did not push me to be perfect. That was all on me. If I counted the number of times I cried in full-out mental breakdowns because I did not make an A, we'd be here for a while.

As school got harder, it started getting increasingly difficult for me to keep all high grades. I started to notice that my science grades and math grades were slowly slipping lower than my history and English grades.

If I made less than a ninety on a test, I would look at myself in the mirror in total disgust and say things like

- You are stupid.
- You are worthless.
- I hate you.

I started spiraling down an endless road of disappointment. It was unrealistic to think I could make 100s on everything. In order to break away from this unhealthy perspective that I had created, I had to realize that you can't be great everything.

It takes a change of focus to heal your "vision" of life.

In tenth grade, I began to have this longing to play basketball again. I had quit a few years ago because it was no longer enjoyable. After nights of pondering the decision, I tried out and made the team!

• • •

My muscles cried out in agony as I pounded forward, sweat flying off my face as I sucked in every bit of air. I begged my eyes not to look away from the line. Ignore the timer. The pressing feeling of my teammates.

None of that mattered.

All I have to do is cross the court sideline before the buzzer sounds. Then all of this would be over. I could feel the timer ticking as the line drew within feet. Taking one last step, the buzzer sounds.

Muscles tearing, heart racing, stomach-turning, I tumbled to the ground.

• • •

In order to achieve success, you must identify one focus and give yourself to it 100 percent. This is because wherever your focus goes, your energy goes. When I focused on being the perfect student, the only thing I was rewarded with was an unsatisfying A.

All that hard work for a letter that society claims represent my worth and ultimate success in life?

As you realize who you want to be, you are going to start to come to some crossroads. You will have to decide between things that will alter where your future goes. Should you switch schools or not? Should you take the honors class or not? Start a side hustle or not?

As I journeyed through the trials of being on a basketball team, I began to realize who I wanted to be versus who I was. As a result, I understood I couldn't do it all.

Slowly, my focus changed from grades to basketball.

Being a competitive person, I wanted to be the all-star player on my team. I already had the defense; I was the girl who would give her all. Diving for balls, getting knocked out, or launching into the stands. If I didn't leave the court bruised, I hadn't given my all. (Sorry, to the vent I destroyed . . . iykyk.)

But I struggled on the offense. I knew in order to improve my game I had to become a shooter. To do this meant letting go of my free time and spending less time on my studies.

The one thing you have to keep in mind is that I did not drop my grades and become a C student. I simply allowed myself to do my best and be content with what I received.

To reach my goal of becoming a shooter, I had to learn the skills of commitment, determination, and focus.

Commitment:

I spent more than ten extra hours in the gym per week outside of our practices.

I was either shooting threes, weightlifting, or dribbling.

Determination:

Even though I had an issue with my leg that had the potential to slow me down, I never allowed myself to fail my coach's expectations. If I did not leave the court purple, blue, and bleeding, I had not played with my entire heart.

Focus:

On the court, my focus was on the ball.

The crowd did not matter.

My negative teammates did not matter.

My only goal was to get my hands on the ball. That way, I could position myself to make the next best decision for my team. The way I look at focus is like a magnifying glass. If you try to look at everything at once, it all seems like a blur. But tune in on one thing, and then everything becomes clear.

Unfortunately, no one ever saw—other than my coach, my family, and my team—my transformation from a sole defensive player to a girl who could do threes like it was nothing because the year 2020 struck, and my focus changed once again.

CHALLENGE FIVE

PUSHING THROUGH THE PAIN (GOALS)

> Venture outside your comfort zone.
> The rewards are worth it.
>
> —Rapunzel (*Tangled*)

Toward the end of 2019, I started to find a true passion in writing. I already knew that I loved writing. I had been doing it ever since I could remember—journaling, song writing, short stories, etc.

You know that one person who writes an entire essay on the birthday card for literally everyone? That's me.

Reading and writing flows through me like the breath of life. One of my favorite memories is when I was in third grade. I was absolutely obsessed with the *Nancy Drew* (an amateur sleuth) series. Nancy was my first role model that I can remember. She was everything I wanted to be and more: strong, fearless, wise, and beautiful inside and out. To all my avid readers, did you ever hide your books under your pillow so you could read after your mom tucked you in?

Ok, don't tell, but that was me every night. I laugh as I think about this, but there was one night when my mom told me I could read until eight o'clock.

• • •

Silence surrounded me. My eyes were heavy, but my mind was racing. Nancy swiftly charging to save the little girl on the cliff unfolded before me as I read from the pages of the all-too-familiar yellow book.

Would Nancy save the girl from the fast-approaching vehicle, or would she fall to her death? I could not read fast enough.

Reality hit for a second. *What time was it?*

Glancing toward my door, my mom hadn't come to check on me yet, so I had a good ten minutes.

Moments later, the satisfying sound of shutting the book filled my ears.

Hey! I finished the book, and it wasn't even eight o'clock yet!

Jumping out of bed, the chilly floor embraced my feet as I rushed to go tell my mom about everything I had just read. Opening the door slightly, I listened.

That's strange.

No one was making a sound.

Tiptoeing into my mom's room, I glanced at the clock. *It was one in the morning!*

Turning back as quickly as possible, I flew back into bed before anyone had a chance to catch me.

• • •

As you can see, even from a young age, I craved something that would become a part of my future.

When you were younger, what was that one thing that you could do for hours?

Where did your imagination take you?

Who or what did you want to become?

Watching my dad go through the process of publishing his book, *Unlocking Your Divine DNA*, inspired me. I admired the commitment he took building connections with the people around him. He allowed himself to become vulnerable so he could help other people.

If my dad had given up and had decided that writing his book wasn't worth it, I would not be sitting here writing my second book.

My dad was part of my foundation in writing, allowing me to dream a dream I never knew I had. Every day, I aspire to make him proud, whether it's working on both of our next projects, picking up a heavier set of weights so I can compete with him, or cooking him a delicious meal. No matter where our paths take us, I know my dreams will align with my dad because he believes in me, and I believe in him.

After my dad had published his book in 2018, I started thinking about the possibility of becoming an author. The idea of young readers reading my books into the depths of the night, just as I had once done with Carolyn Keene (the set of ghostwriters who wrote Nancy Drew), drove my passion.

Sitting down one day, I began to write. My imagination hit the tracks like a bullet train. When I get into my flow, I can write for hours at a time. It took me five months of complete determination and hard work to knock out my first manuscript of *Teenfluencer Nation*.

When I find my reason to write a book, it becomes my sole obsession.

Writing *Twin Tales*, for me, was my way of overcoming my past bitterness that had revolved around people crushing my dreams. When I held the print copy in my hands for the first time, it was like a weight from the past had lifted from me. I no longer had to hold on to the things people had done to me, whether that was old relationships with friends, the church, or mentors.

When you are writing a book, you spend more time rewriting and reworking portions than almost anything else.

And once you are finished writing, you are nowhere near being done with your book. There is a bucketload of other things you must do to accomplish it—marketing, interior/exterior design, illustrations, proposals, etc.

Most people don't realize all it takes for a dream to come true!

It took over a year of learning from my dad and a program I went through called Author Academy Elite to make my dream a reality. (Perhaps you have a dream of writing a book; reach out to me, and I can help you.)

Don't let time nor age be the reason you close the door on your dream. Instead, commit to finding the right resources and mentors that will allow your dream to come true.

When I was writing, publishing, launching, and marketing *Twin Tales*, life did not stop. I still had school, basketball, church, friends, clubs, and family.

You have to make the choice of what is important to you.

For me, I decided that I would not use social media for pleasure. I chose not to scroll endlessly on Instagram. Now, you may be laughing because you think there is no way that could be true. Society has made social media a source of acceptance, a place where people live their "lives," and a tool people "can't" live without.

For myself, I had to create boundaries. This meant using Instagram and Facebook solely as a means to connect with people who align with my core purpose, inspire others, and share my message.

To do this meant

1. creating time limits on the apps.
- This allowed me to assess how long I was scrolling vs. how long I was creating.
2. being self-aware of what I was looking at.

- Was this post or the person I am following making me feel positive, or do I feel negative about myself every time I see this person or this type of post? Aka hitting the unfollow button was sometimes necessary.
- Am I, by posting this, giving value to someone else's life?
- If my dream mentors saw what I am saying or doing on social media, would they be impressed?

Fast forward to 2021. I became the social media director for my high school's student council, I work for one of my dream mentors on social media, I run the social media pages for my favorite place to eat and study, and I work for my publisher.

You'll see that I am regularly active on social media when it comes to going live, posting inspirational posts, and trying hard to connect with the people who have chosen to follow me. I absolutely love creating and investing my time in social media because it is a way for me to express myself and create lifelong connections.

I don't care if I have 500 or 100,000 followers.

Why?

Because if you can change one person's life, then that starts a chain reaction that has the potential to change billions of lives. It changes everything when you think in terms of "life currency" rather than "cash currency."

Ask yourself—is social media impacting you, or are you making an impact through social media? Are you being influenced, or are you the influencer?

Everything can be used for good or evil, and it's up to you to decide.

Is social media distracting you from your future?

Do you feel depressed every time you close the app?

Then I advise you to take a break from it all. Find someone, such as a trusted mentor, to help you detox your social media. Allow them to help you unfollow and block certain things.

Why is that so important?

Because what you see goes straight into your heart and mind. You have to be wise because you can easily begin to sow seeds of lies and misconceptions that can lead to death.

Death to the person you are meant to be.

Death to relationships.

Death to your dreams.

Set boundaries, and learn to look for the good; then the pure joy of life will be your reward.

CHALLENGE SIX

UNDERNEATH THE SMILE (AUTHENTICITY)

> Miracles happen every day. Change your perception of what a miracle is, and you'll see them all around you.
>
> —Jon Bon Jovi

Sometimes when you see someone constantly smiling, always having fun, who has the best grades, or has a rock star body, it can be easy to forget that we all struggle on the inside.

No matter how small or big the problem is, it can be scary. Especially when it seems we must face it all alone.

Your parents could be arguing right now, threatening to separate. You could have failed your last couple of tests, even though you've spent hours studying.

And now you think, *could something be wrong with me?*

Perhaps you woke up one morning, and your life completely changed. Maybe a tragedy—or two—derailed your life.

That happened to my family at the beginning of 2020. We had been going through a bumpy season. There were unexpected deaths, I had changed schools three times, we were in the process of moving, and my mom was facing health issues.

In February, my sister was rushed to the hospital in the middle of the night because her blood sugar was over six hundred. If you did not know, one's blood sugar should be around 70–120. Six hundred means that one could go into a coma at any moment and perhaps even die.

While my sister was fighting for her life in the ICU, I was asleep. I had no idea any of this was happening until I woke up the next morning to hear that my sister was in the hospital. When we went to see her, she had been moved a couple of times due to the severity of the situation. It was heartbreaking seeing her lying there confined to the hospital bed.

It frustrated me.

I hated being unable to do anything.

When the doctors told us she had Type One Diabetes, we immediately rebuked it because we believed she would be healed. To this day, we say she was diagnosed with Type One Diabetes, not that she has it.

Even the slightest words have power.

Type One Diabetes is not something you can keep from getting. The doctors don't know exactly why it happens. Some say it's genetic, while others say it's due to stress or a virus.

On the outside, Makena looks normal. No one would know that she has to take shots every time she wants to eat or that she has to constantly monitor her blood sugar to make sure it's not too high or too low. Even the beeping sound of her alarm causes her embarrassment during her classes at school.

In reality, if we make one mistake with her, then death is right around the corner.

However, we do not live in fear.

Each of us has a destiny for greatness, and the journey at times may seem unfair. I have never lived knowing what it's like to have an illness like Type One Diabetes, but I have seen my sister live with it every day.

I have seen her broken.

I have seen her fight.

I have seen her conquer.

And it breaks my heart, and I wish I could take away her heartache, her anger, and her pain. But I can't. All I can do is try to be there for her when she needs me.

Let me assure you that God would never let you face something you can't handle. Now, when it comes to my sister's situation, there is one thing she said while lying on the hospital bed that amazes me.

When we were told that there is no current cure for Type One, my sister said, "I don't want God to *just* heal me. I want to face this in order to find a cure. That way, no other kid has to fight this again."

Makena truly is my hero.

• • •

What are you struggling with that if you overcome it, you could be a light for someone else?

It could be an intense eating disorder. Or your parents are divorced. Your best friend could have left this life unexpectedly.

We all have different trials that we have to face. But we look those trials in the eye, and we gain W's and L's. And no matter what, we come back fighting harder than ever.

• • •

Another person that fought something horrific as a teen is the amazing Bethany Hamilton-Dirks. On October 31, 2003, Bethany, at the age of thirteen, had gone out on the beach to surf. Little did she know that day would change the course of the rest of her life.

As she sat on her surfboard waiting for a wave, she suddenly felt a jolt in her arm, and then the water around her transformed into crimson red. She had been bitten by a shark, losing her left arm.

Some people in this same situation would have given up, but Bethany fought. Not only did she survive the night, but she lived to surf again. And to this day, she surfs, speaks, and has a beautiful family.

If you are struggling with a disability, understand that you will make it. You are writing a story that will help someone else someday.

Yes, people will make fun of you because they don't understand you. In many ways, they may be intimidated by the power you possess.

Keep fighting, have faith, and believe in the fact that you will make an impact on the world. You are a Teenfluencer.

CHALLENGE SEVEN

UNANSWERED QUESTIONS (FAITH)

> It's a lot easier to take a hateful comment when you are living for something bigger than you.
>
> —Sadie Robertson

Examine what's in your heart and make sure your words align with it.

I mentioned earlier that I have an issue with my leg. To give you more context, it looks almost like a port-wine stain, but it's not. It has something to do with the blood flow in my lower left leg. Anytime the temperature changes from cold to hot rapidly, it feels as if a thousand needles are stabbing my leg. It will go numb at times and change colors from a deep purple to firefly red.

Interestingly, I was not born with it. When I was two years old, I had a temperature of 104 degrees, causing a febrile seizure. A day later, a small red spot appeared on my leg.

As the years have gone by, it has slowly spread.

Since I was seven, doctors have been trying to figure out what it is. Professionals have administered laser treatments, MRIs, and many other things. No doctor has any clue what it may be.

It's frustrating when you listen to a doctor talk for more than an hour using medical terms you don't understand, just to hear that they have never seen anything like this and aren't sure how to help you.

There is no worse feeling than being clueless and helpless. At some point in life, we get tired of people saying, "I do not know, and we just need to run more tests."

About a year ago, a doctor asked me what I wanted from him. What I said was, "I just want an answer."

• • •

I know that in many areas of my life, I have questioned and begged for answers.

Unsurprisingly, mankind cannot supply them all.

When someone we love dies, we want to know *why*.

When we are diagnosed with an illness, we want to know *why*.

Why *me*?

Why *now*?

Why *this*?

The emotions that come with an inexplicable why can tear us down until we feel no more.

Have you ever felt that dreaded numb feeling of uncertainty that sneaks up on you in the middle of the night?

I know I have, and sometimes after a hard day and lonely night, I can feel it creeping back.

Where do you go when it seems like there's no safe place to turn?

Some time or another, we have to realize that not all answers are found in man. There are answers that can only be found in God. And sometimes, his answers aren't what we want to hear.

• • •

When I was younger, I was bullied because of the issue with my leg. The bullying season was the greatest when I had the laser treatment done because I was not allowed to go outside and risk exposure to the sun's rays.

People of all ages, from three to 80, would look shocked when they caught a glimpse of my leg, asking in some way or another, "OMG! What happened to your leg?"

Total embarrassment is how I reacted in these situations. I would shut down and mumble something about how I had a seizure, and the red spots appeared as a result.

Then people gasp, "Does it hurt?"

That's the moment when more people would start to take notice of the conversation. People weren't always trying to be rude or mean but were genuinely curious. However, being so young, I did not understand that. I never wanted anyone to see it, nor did I tell anyone about it unless they asked.

I've tried to cover it up with makeup, which only results in the makeup getting all over my clothes.

When I play basketball, I wear compression socks because it slightly reduces the pain in my leg. The funny thing is, even in a world of injured players, people made fun of my socks!

I mean, come on, *who has the time to care what type of socks someone is wearing?*

Up to this point, I don't have a success story to share. I still have the issue with my leg. There was even a point where I honestly thought that I was healed. I had made up my mind that it was just a bruise, but as of now, the stain is still on my leg.

However, I don't let that condition rule me anymore. If I could get rid of it, I would. But for right now, it is something that makes me different and unique, plus it has taught me how to push through the pain. I have chosen not to allow others to influence me but to use my pain to influence others in a positive way.

"The 20-meter pacer test will begin in 30 seconds. Line up at the start. The running speed starts slowly but gets faster each minute after you hear this signal. BEEP."

It felt like needles pressed against my skin as I ran to the opposite side of the court, determined to beat the sound. It was the forty-third lap of the pacer test. I was the only girl remaining, and I was determined to beat the three other boys that were left.

Shock filled my eyes as my feet slipped from under me. Pounding to the ground, my knees burned like fire. Stumbling to get back up, I pushed myself off the court floor and continued to run.

What just happened?
BEEP.
Ahhh. I missed it.
Frustration fueled my body. *I had only one more strike left!*

Turning around, I focused on the next lap. I was no longer motivated to beat the boys, but I was determined to catch back up with the pacer.

Just as I pushed off my back leg to keep running, I felt lines of pain striking through my knee.

(I ignored it, of course, which I would come to do in every basketball game and practice from that day forward.)

Two boys gave up, leaving just me and the other boy.

By this time, I could not feel my left leg or the tops of my knees. I could tell I was slowing down.

Five feet behind my opponent, I could hear the sound of the timer approaching. I lunged with all my strength toward the court line. *BEEP!*

Only a few seconds separated me from my victory.
I lost.
(Or so I thought.)

• • •

After that day, I knew I could do whatever I put my mind to. Yes, in reality, I lost the race to a guy who ran track. But I also beat thirty other guys and girls. Plus, my friends got to push me in a wheelchair around the school for more than two weeks because I had bruised all the tissues in my right and left knees.

Little did I know that each time I would leave the court after a competitive event, I would leave with a bruised knee. The same experience was repeated when I was on my high school basketball team, and my coach would make us run laps.

My left leg would kill me, perhaps because we had been running suicides for an hour. Every time I made it to the line, I would kneel on the floor, rubbing my leg, trying to get circulation back.

This time, however, I never let the buzzer sound before I was across the line. I never gave in to the temptation to quit, letting myself and my team down.

This time, I pushed all the way through and ran until the buzzer sounded. I earned the respect of my coach and the unexpected respect of my teammates. Respect was earned not from my words but my actions.

Sharing my struggle is a risk. What will my readers think? Will they quit reading and move on to another author?

The reason I am telling you all of this is because I want you to realize that we all have things we are embarrassed about or hate about ourselves.

We *all* have reasons to quit.

Yet, each moment of suffering creates an opportunity to learn. What do you learn from quitting?

Aren't you ready to break past the barrier of "I quit" and step into the land of "I conquered?"

When people are bullying you, don't lower yourself because of them. In reality, their goal is to see you suffer because they suffered and did not win.

I am calling you up and cheering you on to run the next lap. Keep walking with your head up. You are stronger than the words they are speaking into you, and you are greater than any medical issue that might consume you. Learn from your past experiences and allow them to give you wisdom for the trials you will face in the future. Be a Teenfluencer!

CHALLENGE EIGHT

BIGGER THAN ME (SERVICE)

> We can't help everyone,
> but everyone can help someone.
>
> —Ronald Reagan

I want you to look yourself in the eye and embrace your greatness. Yes, greatness often starts at the bottom. Nevertheless, this is the path to the top. Seeing themselves as a failure is one of the reasons most people never pursue their dreams.

When I played basketball in tenth grade, I crowned myself honorary water girl. Whenever I was not on the court, I laid aside my pride and filled up water bottles for my teammates, who treated me like trash.

The bottom certainly doesn't feel good.

The girls I was serving would literally spit the water back in my face. They did not have my back. Nevertheless, I had chosen to have their back because they were my team.

As I served, I caught the attention of the adults around me. My coach respected me more than any of the star players on the team. As a result of my earned respect, he offered me personal training time every morning.

Serving opens doors you never knew existed beforehand. It's not easy to let go of your pride and desire to fit in, but when you serve those whom you have a right to hate, you will take a step closer to who you are meant to be.

Another way of serving is to sacrifice a part of your time to show people you care. Sometimes simply listening demonstrates you are there.

In today's age, we can get so involved going through life living in a world under the spell of the internet that we let the physical world pass us by.

I challenge you to be intentional as you listen to the people around you.

It may be that you hear that a friend loves to play golf. Sure, you may not enjoy golf, but your friend does. So, you take a day out of your week to take your friend to Top Golf. This shows that you are observant and you truly understand your friend.

A personal example I have is that I knew a girl at my school who was having a rough week. We weren't friends, but I knew her birthday was on Monday. I overheard her say once that she really loved the breadsticks from Olive Garden.

So, *what did I do?*

I bought her some breadsticks from Olive Garden and gave them to her on her birthday.

When she saw what I had done, she was in total shock and couldn't speak. The bell rang for class, and she smiled a thank you and then raced off to class.

Did we ever speak again?

No.

Not all relationships end in friendship.

Our lives have never crossed paths again, but all I can hope is that when she goes to Olive Garden, she remembers that there's someone out there who cares enough about her to listen to even the simplest things she has to say.

Is there someone in your life you could empower through serving?

I am calling upon you to take that risk and do something humbling for that person this week.

Trust me, it will change your life, and it will leave an impression on the life of the other person. Teenfluencers leave their mark on the world.

CHALLENGE NINE

PART OF THE SOLUTION (PARTICIPATION)

> It's not enough to be against something.
> You have to be for something better.
>
> —Tony Stark (*Captain America: Civil War*)

As you grow up, you quickly find out that the world does not revolve around you. Life is going to throw curveballs at you no one ever sees coming. You could get in a car wreck, a close relative could pass away, or you could even go blind.

As I mentioned earlier, one of the curveballs of life that greatly impacted me was when my sister was diagnosed with Type One Diabetes.

At that time, I was attending Blue Lake Academy. It was an amazing school. I loved the opportunities this school gave me.

However, Blue Lake does not have a band, and my sister was already fully invested in the Turtle Rock High School band. There was no way she would give up this part of her life.

For me, I would survive without the extra college credits, but my sister, on the other hand, could not survive without music. Knowing that there was no way I would let her go into the school that had chewed me to pieces my freshman year, I decided to make another life-altering decision. This time it was not for my happiness; it was for my sister.

Life is made up of many things we may not like, and making sacrifices for the ones we love is part of it.

Late one night, I lay in bed as tears fell from my eyes.

I could not decide whether to leave another school, only to return to the place that I had intentionally left earlier. Deep down, I knew that I was bitter. Furious and hurt by that school, I couldn't even think about it without feeling disgusted.

I hated the smell of it.

The way it looked.

To me, it was a giant "pretty" green box containing a whole lot of disappointment.

That night, the answer I knew but did not want to hear came from God. It was time for me to return.

Did I want to?

No.

Even though that same night I told my mom and my most trusted friend what I was thinking, I kept it a secret from everyone else for almost three months.

I was absolutely terrified of returning until one day, I learned to forgive. Teenfluencers learn to let go of hurts and forgive the people who have hurt them.

• • •

Sitting down, I stared at the empty notebook in front of me. What I was about to do was the only thing I could think of doing. My emotions, like a rope, tightened like a knot within me. The pain, the anger, and the frustrations threatened to explode at any moment.

Taking a deep breath, I grabbed my pencil and began to write and write and write.

I wrote everything down, from what I had expected at Turtle Rock High School to the truth about what actually happened.

- Bullying from teachers and students
- Miscommunication and bad information
- Unprofessionalism
- And more

Slowly, as I turned to the fourth page, I took a deep breath. Here came the hard part, forgiving and moving forward.

The next page of my emotional letter consisted of my goal to create a better environment inside my school that was just as beautiful as the outside. It does not matter how pretty something looks; it's the inside that counts. I promised in that letter that I would be a part of the change. Three days later, I read this six-page letter to the principal of my freshman year school.

I was terrified. My entire body shook, and my voice was slightly unsteady in that large conference room.

Yet, I spoke with confidence and assurance because I knew if I did not share my heart, there would be no chance for a change.

When I left that office, I sent an email to the Student Council leader asking how I could become a part of the student leadership. One hour later, they asked if I could come to the school to help out with freshman orientation. I accepted.

And with that, the journey back to where I started two years ago began. The only difference in the scenario this time was me. In that moment, I chose to be the influencer rather than the influenced.

• • •

Walking into my old school again as a student was such an odd feeling. My heart raced, not in excitement nor in fear, but in wonder. Curiosity filled my mind.

How would people react to the fact that I was back?

Would they even remember me?

I turned down A Hall and walked past the hundreds of other students finding their place on the first day of school.

The complicated and diverse group of teens around me burdened my heart. I caught glance after glance of eyes full of panic, fear, uncertainty, and emptiness. No one had any idea how this year would be. It was the first time anyone had been anywhere with this number of people in months, thanks to quarantine.

Sitting down at a table, I smiled.

This was going to be a year like no other. It was going to be hard. It was going to be frustrating. But it was a place where I could stand out as a light to all who were around me. Yes, I would stand out in a world pressing in.

• • •

Walking through an old door with a new heart, I understood that if I wanted a different reality, I was the only factor in the equation that could control in order to get a different result.

And this time, I was different. I had confidence in who I was. I no longer needed anyone to make me feel accepted because I understood that I am not meant to fit in with the crowd.

During the eleventh grade, I got to be there for my sister, and I would never take it back. There were times when I actually was able to keep her from going to the hospital.

For instance, her sugar had gotten so low that she was shaking and unable to think. At that moment, I was two doors down from her classroom and got the URGENT LOW ALERT on my phone. I was able to grab some juice for her and get her to the nurse before anything went tragically wrong.

During that year, I kept people in their place when they were trying to bully my sister or her friends. No, I didn't get physically into fights or punch kids, but I worked magic in the background to make sure that the right authority put them in their place.

As older siblings know, you can mess with me, but you cannot mess with my siblings. *I* am the only one allowed to do that.

While at Turtle Rock High School my eleventh grade year, I got an experience that I would never take back, such as being the social media director at my school. This truly helped with becoming confident in my own skin and enhancing my skill set because I was going live on Instagram every day.

(Yes, if you look hard enough, you may find some of those videos—even the videos from my first business—are out there to be found.)

Why haven't I deleted them?

I want you to can see the growth and the potential you have if you take a risk and give yourself time.

That year, I completely stepped out of the mindset of being consumed by grades. I truly expressed my own style (which honestly feels like it changes every day), I learned how to juggle about four billion jobs (thank God for Google Calendar), and I did my best to enjoy life all the time.

Now, I am not going to lie to you and say that I am confident 24/7 or that I love school. Actually, I don't get excited when I have to sit in a classroom all day long learning things I probably won't ever use again—cough cough—precalculus.

So, let's pause for a minute because I don't want to skip over this section and leave you thinking I had a perfectly fantastic eleventh-grade year.

No, I did not.

Remember, I did not want to be at this school, but it's where God placed me. I had several emotional breakdowns over Precalculus. I seriously had to retake every single test because if I did not, I would have failed that class.

Precalculus was the first class I ever prayed to get at least a B. It kicked my tail getting that B.

On top of the academic struggle, I only had one real friend. Plus, it sucked having to social distance and wear a mask all day.

At the end of the year, I was treated with great disrespect. I watched my well-deserved position in leadership get taken from me. I worked 80-plus hours growing the social media platform and creating a system that would push the school to a whole new level. And I was demoted. I was more than qualified yet not "popular" enough.

I learned that no matter what an organization's mission statement is, leadership determines what the organization actually does.

If you allow your staff to cuss, students will cuss.

If you do not fund the arts, students with artistic talents won't come.

If you do not have a diverse representation of ethnicities in leadership roles, you will not have diversity represented by your students.

During this season of life, it was my responsibility to get my schoolwork done to the best of my ability on time. I strived for good grades but not perfection. I strived to be involved in school but not consumed.

Your priorities and goals are going to change every year, and you have to learn to be okay with that. It won't always be what you want or think is supposed to happen, but sometimes God is showing you that the challenge is part of your mission, and he is preparing to move you to your best next step.

If I had gotten the position on the council, I would have remained at that school, and my life would look a lot different. Reflecting on the couple of months that followed, I feel blessed that that opportunity went out the window.

God always has so much more in mind, even when we can't see what it is yet. Teenfluencers are patient during the storms.

CHALLENGE TEN

AROUND THE CORNER (UNCERTAINTY)

> We all take different paths in life, but no matter where we go, we take a little of each other everywhere.
>
> —Tim McGraw

As I write this sentence, my world could change tomorrow.

As you read this sentence, your world could be altered next week.

I've learned to allow my passions, dreams, and aspirations to fuel my day. I am not always perfect. I have bad days, just like everyone else. But I am always learning more about who I am every day.

Daily, we have to make decisions.

Daily, we have things we are going through and working to overcome.

I want to be totally transparent with you.

As I wrote this book, there were times when I wanted to stop. I wasn't sure if it really mattered. I've doubted my writing skills. I have doubted myself. But the call in my heart begins to pull at me.

This book isn't just about me. It's also about you.

I have a passion to see you succeed in what you are called to do.

I have a passion to build connections and relationships with teens all over the world. I don't want my life to revolve around me or the fear of the unknown. I want my life to be set up so I can help you step up into your future.

Imagine what we could do as a nation of teens, pushing each other into our next. The connections, the relationships, the opportunities would multiply ten-fold (or maybe I should say "teen-fold").

I don't know what I am going to eat tomorrow or where I will be living by the end of the year. Life is always changing.

There are so many decisions that we make every day that it can be overwhelming. We never know what tomorrow may bring because God always seems to have something up his sleeve. I can assure you, though, that he will never let you face something that he thinks you can't make it out of. And God always has your best interest in mind.

God will answer your prayers.

It may not look like what you thought, and it might be half a decade later, but, in his timing and in his way, God will provide.

In the past few months, as I have been writing this book, God has been answering prayers that I have been praying for since seventh grade.

After years of isolation, God has given me three legendary, fantastic, absolute blessing, abundant, and God-focused friendships. They didn't show up like a lightning strike from Heaven; rather, it was subtle. A series of unbelievable events made it evident that God was involved.

God blessed me with these friendships at a time when I felt unqualified, and I could never feel more content. There is no longer a need to be desperate. My friendship gap is not satisfied. You are going to have to have to be absent from things for long periods of time before you can truly honor and appreciate life.

The amazing thing is that once I release this book, I'll have more opportunities and experiences that will expand my life. I'll be in a different season of life. Perhaps I'll even get to meet you.

The thing is that life is always changing, and we have to be flexible and prepared to change with it. You have to keep your focus even when your position changes.

Now that you know more of what I've faced, I hope you can see that you are not alone. We are all facing challenges in life that are shaping us into who we will become.

My goal is to be authentic with you because I want you to do the same. I am tired of the lies of perfection that the world is putting on our generation.

Influences are pressing in on us. It is time to rise up and stand out. Be a leader. Take your place as a Teenfluencer. It's time to come together as a nation of teens who are the influencers, not the influenced. In the next portion of this book, I am going to break down what it takes to truly become a Teenfluencer and how we are going to do it *together*.

PART 2

12 CHARACTERISTICS THAT TEENS NEED

What exactly is a Teenfluencer?

If you are a teen (ages thirteen to nineteen) and you are influencing someone or something in your life, then you are classified as a Teenfluencer.

Teenfluencers are represented by teens who have written a book, run their own bakery, started a photography business, model in the fashion industry, are a baseball star, a pageant queen, run their own blog, volunteer for the homeless, babysit, work a job, provide for their family, are a big or little sister, coach and train in fitness, are the founder of a club, are a speaker, a hardworking student, etc.

The opportunities today to create influence are endless. The phone in your hand becomes a key that can open a door where you can make an impact.

The question is, *what* type of impact are you making?

You have the potential to leave a positive and lasting impact wherever you go, whether that is playing your part in a group project or the fact that your smile shifts the atmosphere in the room.

The words you speak, the way you represent yourself, and where and who you devote your time to have the power to influence and change someone's life.

On the other hand, you also have the power to destroy your life and reputation, along with someone else's, through a single post online.

Your *online* presence is just as impactful, perhaps even more so than your *in-person* one. As a teen, you can reach millions of people within seconds online, and if you present yourself as impure, negative, or a fake, your adult reputation will be affected.

When you attend your ten-year reunion at your high school, what will people say about you?

Will they question your success because you used to be negative to everyone?

Or will they remember you because you sat with every new kid at school and were always so kind to everyone?

Being a positive Teenfluencer is an honor and a burden. You have to separate yourself from the crowd. You will be challenged for your decisions. You will make mistakes, and you will have to own up to them. *You will have to stand out even when the world is pressing in.*

BUT.

You will also have doors opened to you unlike any other. You will reap the reward of bringing joy to someone's life. And you will live a life of passion and certainty because you will know you are on the path that for which you were created.

Teenfluencers have existed as long as teens have been around—from the teenage Queen Esther, who saved her entire kingdom by risking her life, to Michael Jackson, who grew up as a teenage pop star legend, to Bethany Hamilton, who learned to surf again after she lost her arm in a shark attack.

Living the present-day life of a teen is completely different from what life looked like for our parents, not to mention our grandparents. We live in a world of instant obtainment.

We can learn anything we want in seconds. Our parents, on the other hand, had to wait an entire week before watching the next episode of their favorite show. Gasp!

Here are some examples of how our lives differs from our parents':

Our Parents—Source Of Games
    Imagination
    Some toys
    Non-electronic board games
    The first set of video games
    Weekly TV specials
    Average amount of screen time: 0–2 hours

Teens Today—Source Of Games
    iPhones = any online game
    Laptops = any online game
    Virtual Reality = any online game
    Nintendo Switch = any online game
    Binging any and all Netflix, HBOMax, Disney+, Amazon Prime, etc. shows
    Imagination
    Average amount of screen time: 9+ hours

Our Parents—Education
    Fewer than five hours a week of homework
    Twenty or fewer classes to choose from
    Homeschooled, public, or private
    Learning platform: printed textbooks

Teens Today—Education
    More than seven hours a week of homework
    The options are endless
    Public, online, hybrid (public and online), EL education, Common Core, private, or homeschooled
    Learning platform: iPads, computers

Recap
The core difference between our two realities as it relates to the way we play, learn, and overall live. The teens of today have more options and choices to choose from.

I don't know about you, but just thinking about it gives me a feeling of anxiety.

Every day, our brain makes around 35,000 decisions, with over two hundred of them being food alone. Now, these decisions start from the moment we wake to the moment our head hits the pillow at night.

Some of the biggest decisions we make as a teen are when we must choose our class schedule for the following year. Personally, every year when it comes to selecting my classes, I always wait till the last minute because there are so many classes to choose from, and it makes my brain hurt.

The school systems seem to support the narrative that if you pick one wrong class, your entire educational future as you know it could be altered. Plus, even if you pick a class that you really like, there's no guarantee that you will get in, even though you spent a whole week praying about which classes to pick. Then there are three or four teachers who teach that same class, so you don't even know if you will get a nice teacher.

Our parents had a limited number of ways to spend their time. We have the blessing and the curse known as seemingly endless choices. We can watch an extra hour of TV or hit the gym. We can stay inside all day or choose to go outside for a reading session. We can order any type of food we want from any restaurant we please, and it will be at our door within the hour.

Peer pressure, hours of homework, future plans, family burdens, etc., mean we have to learn what it takes to have patience, prioritize time, and truly work hard. If we don't, our generation will fail.

You cannot achieve your dreams by sitting on the couch thinking about what you might want to do.

You have to get out and experiment.

You have to study and learn about the things that interest you. You have to get to know yourself. As you explore your interests, you will discover your genius. This pursuit will be both positive and negative.

The good.

The bad.

And the ugly.

Choose not to lie down on your pillow at night and feel unaccomplished. You are worth so much more. We can change the world together. I am calling you to join the Teenfluencer Nation and be part of the solution. *How do we get there?*

No one person can do it alone, but we have to get alone in order to make a difference to the "man [or woman] in the mirror." In the next part of this book, we are going to dive deep into what it takes to become a Teenfluencer.

Are you ready?

CHARACTERISTIC ONE

IMPACT

You're braver than you believe, and stronger than you seem, and smarter than you think.

—Christopher Robin (*Winnie the Pooh*)

Who are you?
Who am I?
These are questions that every human being will be confronted by at some point in their life. We become so consumed with becoming a person of the future that we miss who we currently are.
What are you going to do in your life?
What's your calling?
How will you make a change?
What are you going to do that no one else has ever done?
These types of questions flood our minds. Truly they have been pounding at us since we were young. Sometimes, it is from the outer world, while other times, it is from within our own minds. It can become consuming and discouraging when you are plagued with the maybe or a what-if.
Clarity seems so far away at times.
The road to the clear picture can be long and crooked.

It can feel like we never find that step that leads us into our calling. It seems so easy to get stuck in the past, or we can worry about the future.

Living in the present can so be so elusive.

Why?

Why is it so hard to either get stuck in the past or consumed in the thoughts of the future?

I am asking myself too.

It's frustrating.

I don't want to get stuck in the cycle that so many people are trapped in.

Wake up.

Work.

Fight.

Long for something more.

Sleep or lay awake, anxious and unable to sleep.

Life is just too short.

I can find myself thinking there has to be something so much more than this. If life is just this, then what's the point? Why is it so hard for us to miss the big picture and get so consumed by our own lives?

Life is not *only* about us. It is about the impact, inspiration, knowledge, and creativity that you bring to the table. No one in the world has your name or looks just like you.

No one has that scar from when you slammed your head against your grandma's glass table or the slightly bent finger from when you broke it playing baseball.

How'd you do that? They ask.

Well, it was a homerun game-winning hit, but your finger bent the wrong way when you swung the bat. Ignoring the pain, you shot from base to base as fast as a bullet.

At least that's what you are tempted to tell people when they ask.

It definitely was *not* your closet door that you got in a fight with after the baseball game (wink, wink).

My point is that you are one of a kind and unlike anyone else. You have talents you have yet to discover. Take a moment to look up the meaning of your name. Where does your name come from? How does it relate to who you are today, what your past was like, or how might this help you discover what your future may hold?

Names have power, and a lot of us can become so used to people calling us by our name that we lose the rarity and power of our name. Your name brings identity, recognition, reputation, and opened doors. It summons, it informs, it qualifies. It calls to you to be you.

When you call out someone's name, they can tell if it's in urgency, love, hatred, mockery, etc. And their response will evoke the conversation, actions, or few words that follow.

Our name given to us at birth is our first and might just be a label. In reality, your true name identifies who you are and your reason for being. My publisher, Kary Oberbrunner, calls this "your secret name." You are called to walk with great boldness and head held high because you are the (insert your name)!

But somewhere along the way, all of us seem to lose sight of who we are. We get focused on the words spoken over us by people, not God. Our name fades away into just a name, something we've always had. Nothing special. We start to believe those thoughts inside our heads that are not true; those false thoughts can sabotage us for years.

A thought is an idea. It's an opinion, not a fact. Thoughts are produced by thinking and occur suddenly in the mind. Over the past eighteen years, I've had thoughts that I've perceived as truths when they were lies and thoughts that I saw as lies when they were truths.

Here are just a few examples of times when I lost sight and yet, once again, regained focus. I learned a lesson worth more than money can buy.

1. I thought friendship was for life. However, not all friendships are. Some friendships are for a reason, others for a season. And few are for a lifetime.
2. I thought nothing was harder than being betrayed by anyone and everyone you bring close. You have to learn to guard your heart but also know when to let someone in.
3. I thought forgiving someone meant you could reconcile the relationship; it doesn't always end like that.
4. I thought I had to fake a smile and continue to pour into others when I was aching inside. Empty. I believed people didn't like me because I wasn't good enough, and I could never measure up.
5. I thought moving away from everything I had ever known was going to break me. And it did. It tore me, and yet afterward, it brought me strength.
6. I thought my grades, my image, and my imperfections defined me. Hatred. Darkness. Cries. Deep pain. I was my worst enemy. Now, I am learning to love myself in a healthy way.
7. I thought food was the enemy until I had a mentality shift. I learned to see food as fuel and that it can be enjoyed. It takes balance and doesn't require restrictions and rules. Life is too short.
8. I thought exercise was punishment for bad decisions yesterday until I learned it could be used to bring me strength, clarity, balance, and good health. It is actually an investment into the future.

9. I thought obeying God by sitting and standing alone in Him at school would bring me a friend to stand by my side. But it didn't work out like that. I'm not even attending the same school anymore. Years later, I know I have a friend that has my back. God's timing can take over half a decade, but it was worth the wait.

10. I thought moving schools would bring new and good relationships. It brought connections. It brought insight. It brought perspective. It brought humility and the lesson of servanthood. It showed me that leadership will influence the type of people an organization attracts. I learned that a fancy building doesn't determine what's on the inside.

11. I thought that if you work hard, people will want to be a part of what you are doing. I thought tenacity was contagious. Yes, it is sometimes, but a lot of times, people get jealous. They want to put out your flame. The hard work you do doesn't get seen most of the time. Sometimes, people will "spit in your face" after you've finished serving them. But I assure you that someone is watching and that someone might have the power to change your life.

12. I thought I'd never go back to my old school, where I was bullied and mistreated. I returned and thought I had a fresh start, but it still ended in flames. It didn't end the way I had hoped. Yet, this time I finished an assignment. I had been put there to protect my family, and the burns this time around didn't scar because I was protected by God.

13. I thought you were supposed to look perfect when you leave the doorstep of the home because people are watching and judging, but we are all broken and

need healing in some way. No family is perfect. We fight. We cry. We miss each other. Perfection is a lie. We don't look good in every picture. We have laundry that piles up. We have dogs that get into the trash. We don't have a homemade dinner on the table every night of the week. We run late for school. It's called life.

14. I thought God had left me, but I am the one who placed the bricks between me and His people, the Church. He's always been beside me, wiping my tears, and giving me the strength to be patient. To stand alone in Him. And He is there to help me break down the walls.

    I thought people affiliated with the church were all loving until I began to see that some were traitors, liars, deceivers, and users. And I thought every church person was like this. Yet, I learned to trust with wisdom that people can change for better or for worse. That even when you pour your life into someone, that doesn't mean the seed will sprout. I learned there is good and bad in every organization. I learned not to categorize. I learned everything comes back to one's mentality, true intentions, and relationship with God.

    I thought I'd have a senior year with Friday night lights, not spent alone in a crowd of thousands, and dances with people I enjoy being with. I thought I'd be in class finally with a group of kids aligned with my focus. But God had a different plan. He gave me two friends who are now my best friends. He closes doors we think are perfect. Sometimes God reveals His way instantly or and other times, it is years down the road. I've learned to take risks that mean jumping headfirst into experiences that don't always make sense. Being comfortable is not my life. I can't see where I'm going, and every year my direction changes. A new roller coaster loop takes me by surprise. It makes me sick and anxious at times. I don't understand. I can really hate it. But then God reminds me that he's got me. And then it creates a thrill of faith!

15. I thought nothing was harder than being alone. However, it's harder when there's an unwanted space between you and your current relationships. This gap may be physical space geographically or a misconception or miscommunication that's been built up. But time and intentionality can bring you to where you want to be with people who feel distant. Trust the process.

16. The list could go on, and, as I continue to grow up, the list will grow too. Life is what you make it—the good, the bad, the beautiful, and the ugly.

Everybody has thoughts that are built upon perspectives that are one-sided, even when we don't realize it. We can't always see the whole picture, and it can feel as if we are drowning in the deep. It can seem as if the dark winter will never end.

But remember, the season will pass, and another will come. With new seasons come new perspectives, new relationships, new opportunities. Everyone is facing something.

Sometimes it takes listening to someone else's story, being there for someone else, and reaching out to someone for you to overcome a current season and be able to look back and find the beauty of what you went through to become who you are.

Remember, *everything* you endure is for a reason because you are here now for a *reason*.

We all have things we are good at and things with which we need help.

Yes, you have to focus on yourself and your needs in order to step into your next season. Yes, you have to focus on others to step into your next one. Yes, you must focus on God to know how to step into your next time. Focus too little or not enough in one area, and your tower will fall.

Don't be afraid to change your mind from what you once thought as you go through life, read different things, and see different perspectives. And do not be surprised if your thoughts change when the whole picture becomes visual.

CHARACTERISTIC TWO

BELONGING

You can't do your best when you're doubting yourself. If you don't believe in yourself, who will?

—Michael Jackson

Life can be king at throwing you curveballs you were never expecting.

Last year, in the spring of 2020, I had been having some minor back pain. In the past, it mainly happened after a basketball game or intense workouts. This time it was after I had been sitting for a while.

It came to the point where it was a constant annoying pain. No, nothing that was keeping me from doing what I love, but it was painfully annoying, almost like when you have a crick in your neck or a sore muscle.

My mom had a friend who was connected with a scoliosis doctor, and they offered to give my family a screening. At the time, I had never heard of nor knew what scoliosis was. The treatment place was in North Carolina. We scheduled the meeting and drove to the clinic.

My sisters and I were excited about the fact that we would be staying near a Yellow Deli (Literally the best freshly baked bread, granola, and freshly made sandwiches ever! And the setup of the place is so cute. If you haven't been to one, you have to go at least once in your life).

After we got to the scoliosis center, my sisters, my mom, and I had to fill out twenty-something pages about our living environment, diet, etc. It took what felt like a lifetime to fill out! Once we got finished, we went in, talked with the doctor for a couple more *hours*, and got x-rays.

We ended the day with some scrumptious Yellow Deli sandwiches (they are open twenty-four hours a day, five days a week) and headed back to South Carolina.

Three days later, the doctor FaceTimed us to break down our results. To save you all the medical info and big words, I'll just say that both my mom and I were diagnosed with a level of scoliosis that qualified both of us for a two-week treatment. My sister's neck was out of alignment and needed one week of treatment.

When I heard this news, I was upset.

If you don't know what scoliosis is, it's a sideways curvature of the spine. The cause of most scoliosis is unknown. I have no idea how I developed it, nor if it was there when I was young. I can only think that it was the result of getting knocked down and diving so much in basketball and/or sitting at a computer all day and carrying a thirty-pound backpack for school.

When we were diagnosed with scoliosis, it was explained that it would never really go away and is estimated to shorten a person's lifespan by fourteen years. Unless, however, God provides a miracle, which I fully believe he can and will.

When I heard this news, however, I was not peaceful and like, "all is good; God will provide." No, my blood was boiling as my cheeks turned crimson. Thoughts raced through my mind like,

"Why do I strive to live so healthy if it doesn't matter anyway?

What did I do to cause this?

Why should I have to go through pain just to improve something when it can't get better anyway?"

Some of you might understand, but it can be hard to see the positives in life when you hear some bad news. Especially when you are told you have to go through eight hours of treatment every day for *weeks*.

Plus, you are not allowed to lift more than ten pounds for *weeks*. And afterward, you are going to have to wear these gnome-looking weight hats and do this exercise for two hours every day, morning and night.

Now don't get me wrong, I was not dying, but if I don't get this fixed, it could impact my health in the long run, taking decades from my life. For a girl who lifts weights daily and is always on the go, this was a major setback.

Despite this annoyance, my mom, sister, and I pushed through. We committed to the intense treatment and completed it. It was long, exhausting, and extremely boring.

Have you ever stared at a wall so long you have the dents and creases memorized?

I have. Halfway through the scoliosis treatment, we all wanted to quit. Our muscles were sore, our hormones were crazy, and we were just plain tired. We literally sat in the Yellow Deli, crying. Our poor waiter must have thought we were mentally insane.

After the treatment, my results showed slight improvement from x-ray to x-ray. Apparently, I have a strong and stubborn back. When I saw there was little to no improvement, I was frustrated and angry. I didn't understand why my mom and sister were seeing good results, but I did not.

That day, after I had time to process my frustration, I learned that all of us are different. Our bodies respond differently, and sometimes people take a little bit longer to get to where they want to be.

Even in the same family, we have different response times and perspectives. Some people must experiment more to get the right results.

To this day, I still struggle with scoliosis, but I am always working to improve my condition. I have had people declare my healing who didn't even know I had issues with my spine. God hasn't made his move yet, but when he does, it will be known.

We have come to terms with areas where we struggle and give these areas more attention.

It looks different in various areas of life. For me, this might look like wearing a back brace on a back day when I am weightlifting. It also means studying extra for precalculus because if I don't, I will fail, compared to English, where this subject comes naturally to me.

When it comes to basketball, I have to spend hours more dribbling than I do defense. *We all have weaknesses.*

We all have strengths.

Don't be afraid to work harder in an area of life just because you might faceplant while you're at it.

Life is *hard*.

Life is *unfair*.

But *your* life is what you make of it. What are you going to make with the life you have been given?

CHARACTERISTIC THREE

CONFIDENCE

> **You are infinitely more valuable than people's opinion of you.**
>
> —Tauren Wells

How do you support yourself and walk with confidence? How do you keep your fire burning that becomes contagious?

Finding the strength to be confident is one of the hardest things to face. We live in a world where people judge, scrutinize, and hate on anyone who is different or has something worth being jealous of.

In my early years of high school, I was not confident. I did not feel good in my own skin, and I hated asking questions in class. Even within the walls of my own family, I could feel my confidence level being smothered.

When I switched schools and started playing basketball, I began to challenge my confidence level. I did this by throwing myself into what I already had some confidence in—defense. I knew I was more skilled in that area than any of my teammates. I knew that if I could earn their respect by letting them know they could count on me to get the ball back, they would begin to trust me on and off the court.

The group of girls that I played with was mean. They bullied me, stole from me, and hated me because of my skin color. Not to mention, they were so disrespectful and outright rude to my coach.

Now, I never spoke out verbally against their actions, but as I started to gain confidence in my game, I spoke out through my actions. When we would scrimmage, they hated to get me as their defendant because they knew that they would have to foul in order to score.

My defensive game, fueled by confidence that allowed me to dive for balls, launch toward the stands, and rip the ball from an opponent, started flowing into my offensive game. Toward the end of the year, I started calling for the ball and taking more risky ball-handling moves. I went from being conservative on the offensive side of the court to going in for a lay-up. Confidence grows.

The confidence I had found did not stay on the court, but it started to bleed into my personal life. One way I have found to tell if a person is confident or not is in the way they walk. One thing I learned when experiencing different cultures is that a lot of us are in a hurry.

Confidence does not look like a rushed walk but more like a strut. I used to always walk fast, nervous. I'd be late for class. Then, I realized that few teachers marked you late, so why in the world do I need to get worked up over nothing.

I used to be so self-obsessed with the way I looked and dressed that I hated having to walk to the front of the classroom and ask the teacher a question because I *knew* everyone was watching me.

People make comments and take note of everything. The way you look. The sound your shoes make when you walk. The fact that your hair looks a little wild today. But I guarantee you that by tomorrow they will likely have forgotten what you were wearing.

Finding your style is important whether you're a guy or a girl. You don't have to wear the newest trends or styles; in fact, I challenge you to step out of the trend. Who's your biggest inspiration, or what is your favorite decade? Take the styles of that person or era and make it your own. Confidence inspires creativity.

For me, I love to mix up my style every day. Keep the people guessing whether it's what's trending or if it's some '80s-style jacket. In my opinion, the '80s is the best.

If you walked around with your head down, people might make fun of you or never notice you. However, if you walk confidently down the hallway, people notice. They see you have something different. It provokes them to want to ask questions, which opens the doors for you to begin a relationship.

Having confidence can start with small acts that will begin to flow into large areas of your life. Perhaps, confidence will begin with you telling a stranger that you love their shoes. Or it could mean asking a question in class. Or maybe you start a spontaneous dance party wherever you go. Faith it until you make it!

I challenge you to begin to develop confidence in your life. Observe that girl or guy you look up to. What are they doing? What can you learn from their actions? What do they do when they are caught off guard? How do they handle awkward situations?

Next, I challenge you to study someone you admire. Perhaps it's Michael Jackson and his style. If so, start incorporating some Michael Jackson in your own style. No, I am not saying you should wear a full costume and make-up to be confident. Learning from others will help you learn yourself. It is time you own your walk. Go all in.

Oh, why not wear a killer outfit while you're at it?

If you are struggling with confidence, a tip is to wear your clothes like you have been paid to wear them. You may feel like you are wearing the ugliest outfit in the world, but you are getting paid a million bucks, so own it.

You can take this advice and attach it to any area of your life.

• • •

Your name echoes in your head as your teacher nods from the front of the classroom. It's your turn to give your "I believe" speech. You can feel the all too familiar thudding as your heart races. The calculation of the fact that you are only seventy percent ready floods your mind. You wrote your speech, but it sucks. Everyone before you knocked it out of the park.

Well, except Johnathon, who didn't even write his. Oh, and Zoey, who wrote hers on cherry-flavored waffles. Ok, so at least you won't get the worst grade.

Shaking, you walk to the front of the class. Sixty percent of the eyes in the classroom are on you. The others have their attention diverted to phones or to their peers standing outside the window of the classroom.

"Begin," the teacher says sternly. The threatening voice of the one who holds the power to make or break your grade rings through your ears.

No, you tell yourself.

You slam shut the doors of doubt just as they begin to open.

Thinking to yourself ,you ask, *if someone were to pay me a million dollars to give this speech successfully, how would I give it?*

Letting out a deep breath, you toss your script down.

So, what if you mess up a sentence or two. Or heaven forbid, you go off-script. Most people won't notice your mistake anyway. In fact, they might just like what you have to say. It may be a good thing if they weren't bored by the fact that my nose was glued to the script.

• • •

You see, in this scenario, a student is facing the hard task of talking in front of his or her peers.

I know, I still don't like talking in front of peers because peers can be some of the most judgmental people in the world, not to mention you have to see them five times a week for more than eight hours a day.

It can be exhausting trying to be perfect and uphold an image that is impossible to live up to. But if you have confidence in yourself, perfectionism will become less important. Understanding that you have the power to step into a room and claim control is extraordinary.

Before you have the chance to make an impact on a room, however, you have to have the confidence to walk in.

And it all starts with the first step. What step do you need to take?

CHARACTERISTIC FOUR

STANDARDS

Real sacrifice means giving up what you want now for what you want most.
—Tim Tebow

Your muscles pound. Sweat flying. Body aching. You beg your eyes not to look away from the target. Cross the line before the buzzer sounds, and all of this will be worth it. You feel the timer ticking as the line draws within feet. The buzzer sounds as you take one last step, tumbling to the ground.
Did you make it?

• • •

I believe the way to success is to identify one focus and give yourself to it 100 percent. We all have innate dreams, destinies, and purposes, just as we have the need to breathe.

I know how hard it can be to want to do everything. But I also know how unrealistic and self-destroying it can be to do everything.

At one time in my life, I was running a business, playing basketball, leading Student Council, running youth group activities, and taking honors classes. I was able to sustain this for a season, but as things started to pile up, I noticed I was beginning to break down.

I knew I could not do it all, and I was faced with a decision.

I had to dedicate myself to one thing and then position other priorities as second place. For some opportunities, I must learn to say no. What we dedicate ourselves to will change as the seasons of life change. Maybe you realize that you need to dedicate your time and efforts to school, a relationship, or a sport.

In tenth grade, I wanted to be the best basketball player on my team. It was a desire that came from my drive for competitiveness.

I do not like to lose. Does *anyone*?

On the court, as I said before, I struggled on offense. I knew that to improve my game, I had to become a shooter. To do this meant letting go of my free periods that I had been using to study. This extra hour a day gave me one-on-one time with my coach.

On weekdays, I would change from weightlifting and then shoot three-point shots for an hour with my coach.

With no time to change, I would throw off my shooting shoes, throw on some unfashionable yet comfortable Crocs® and race outside into the academic building just in time for chemistry. Drenched in sweat, red as a tomato, I was never late to class, even if that meant running through the rain to go from the gym to the academic building.

It took three months of this routine before I became a three-point shooter. It was worth it, even though I never got to showcase it in a game. My teammates and coach saw my hard work. This commitment paid off.

Now, you might be confused, and you might be asking, "Kiera, if you loved basketball so much and if you practiced so hard to achieve your goals, why did you stop playing basketball after that year?"

Your priorities change.

What you feel deserves your full attention and effort will change.

Personally, when my sophomore year came to an end, I realized that although I loved playing ball, being a basketball player was not who I wanted to be, nor did I have the time to give it my all anymore. I would never take back the moments I had while playing nor the lessons that guided me to discovering who I am.

Through the hardships of the past few years, I have learned that part of my purpose is to empower teens. Slowly, I have eliminated the things that fail to help me toward reaching this aim.

Every day I do the following to achieve my goals:

1. I wake up early. Currently, my goal is 5:00 a.m. Your eyes might have just gotten huge. Why in the world 5:00 a.m.? Well, personally, from 5:00 a.m. to 7:00 a.m., I can get so much done before anyone in my family wakes up. Now, to be honest, I do not wake up at 5:00 a.m. every day. It's hard staying up late because of school, work, or family things. Yet, it is a goal I am working on achieving.

2. I read a devotion and study the Word right when I wake up. This awakens me like nothing else. I can really feel a difference throughout the day if I do not do this.

Right after I do my devotion, I read a chapter in a self-improvement or informational book that I am interested in. For me, the last couple of books I have gone through are *Killing Kennedy* by Bill O'Reilly (I love history involving the

United States presidents), *Unhackable* by Kary Oberbrunner (this is a self-improvement book that is going to shake up your reality; I highly recommend it), and *Raise the Roof* by Pat Summitt (this book I would recommend to anyone. It has so much insight and empowering inspiration from one of the most determined women to have ever lived). Reading daily, even just for ten minutes, feeds the mind. I don't know about you, but when I learn something new that is interesting, I just want to tell everyone. I get so excited!

I have a daily planner that I use to plan out the next day, the night before. In my planner, I have three push goals (I learned this concept from Chalene Johnson) that are going to help me achieve my main goal. In other words, if I only achieve these three goals today, then I will feel accomplished because I took a step toward my next goal. Currently, my main goal is to finish writing this book. So, my current push goals are as follows: 1) do a devotion, 2) write one thousand words, and 3) workout.

Every day, I move. For me, that usually looks like weightlifting because I love how strong I feel after a hard session. On rest days, I either ride my bike with my brother, do a stretch session, or do nothing. Some days nothing is the best therapy.

Working out allows me to let out any inner frustration that I have built up. It allows me to process my thoughts. If I don't work out, I am usually in a not-so-good mood, kind of like when you're *hangry*. Of course, this isn't good for anyone around me.

I try my best to go outside for thirty minutes every day, whether that looks like swimming, reading a good book outside, or riding my bike.

3. Family time. Right now, I have to create family time intentionally, or it will not happen.

In a big family, we all have such busy schedules (my calendar is color-coded by the day). Usually, for our family, since we are so big, all of us are not available to spend time together every single day. Someone is always coming or going. I wish we could, but all we can do is our best.

For us, that looks like planning one night to be with each other. It might look like a Friday night with popcorn, brownies, and a good tv show. (Recently, we have been watching the new Marvel and Star Wars series on Disney+. *Shhhhh*—no spoilers, please!)

> I love to learn, so when I am cooking, driving, or cleaning, I listen to a podcast. My all-time favorite podcast right now is *Build Your Tribe* by Chalene Johnson. It is full of amazing interviews that range from topics about business to health to relationships to living your best life. The podcasts by Parcast Original are good if you're interested in history and unpacking some shocking mysteries! Plus, for all my *Gilmore Girls* fans (#teamjess), Scott Patterson has an epic podcast on interviewing and discussing all things *Gilmore Girls* in his podcast, *I'm All In*.

To achieve something, you have to be determined and dedicated, or time is going to slip past you. You will wake up wishing you could go back to your teen years.

Stop wasting time on social media, boy and girl drama, and family feuds. It's time you set your focus on something and become great at it.

You have the full right to change your mind once you start, but I challenge you to get to a checkpoint. Assess where you went, where you are, and where you're going, and then decide if it's time for you to switch lanes and head down a new path. Remember, Teenfluencers create their world.

CHARACTERISTIC FIVE

FOCUS

> **Never look back. If Cinderella had looked back and picked up the shoe, she would have never found her prince.**
>
> —Selena Gomez

Finding focus and being able to stay away from distractions during your teenage years can be hard. There are so many temptations that are so easily accessible in today's age that tend to be swept under the rug.

Adults tend to not discuss certain things with us because perhaps it makes them uncomfortable, they may have past regrets, or they are blind to the fact that we are faced with such things.

In reality, each day teens are tempted by drugs, alcohol, porn, or sexual activities. Unfortunately, many of us are held captive to these things.

The world can press in on us anywhere. I have stood alone in a locker room with a group of girls who have lost their identities to a spirit of temptation and manipulation, the way they move, the way they speak.

At the time, I felt uncomfortable. The foul language from their tongues and inappropriate movements of their bodies made my skin crawl. I would leave the room as quickly as I could get changed.

Looking back, my heart breaks for them.

Beyond the behaviors they have adopted, there is a girl inside that is broken and searching. Searching for answers that only God can provide.

As a Teenfluencer, we have to be aware of our situation. We must recognize how quickly situations can change.

For example, it's interesting how after an epic win at a basketball game, everyone heads over to the local restaurant for some food. When the hour strikes eleven, more teens tend to arrive.

But this group is a *different* crowd. This group is high, drunk, and has plans for tonight to head over to *the* teen's house whose parents aren't home to do the unspeakable.

This world of temptation is all around us, and we can never get rid of it. But we have to make a choice whether or not to take part in it.

Alcohol is not the answer.

Drugs will not fulfill your brokenness.

Love should not awaken before it is time.

Many of my peers are consumed with chasing after boys or girls. Every month there is a new boy and a new crush. They date for two weeks, get what they want or become bored, and then move on to the next person.

I hear all the time about someone getting pregnant, or someone has overdosed because of something a guy did or a girl said. This is the story of the "influenced."

Why do we value ourselves by whether or not we are with another person?

Why do we feel so empty if we don't have a boyfriend or girlfriend?

For me, the early teenage years are not the time to date and fall in love.

How can we know what we want in a significant other if we don't even know what college we are going to or, better yet, what we want to eat for lunch?

Do you really think you are ready to start pursuing another relationship when you can't even sit through a dinner with your siblings?

The teenage years are the time for us to find out who we really are. It's a time to try things and learn. It is a time for us to discover our identity in this newfound freedom. You have the gift of time. Time to learn an instrument or play a sport. Time to make mistakes and grow. This season of your life offers you a rare opportunity of focusing on yourself. The aim of this time is for you to grow into who you were created to be.

If you are focused on someone else, how can you get to know yourself?

Truly, the only person who I have fallen *in love* with is Jess Mariano (if you've seen the TV show *Gilmore Girls*, you understand). But because I have never been focused on boys, it has allowed me a freedom to direct my focus to other things that are specific to building up who I am so that when the time comes, I will be prepared to build up my future husband.

Time is something everyone at some point in their life wishes they had more of. We all have the same twenty-four hours; the difference between the impactful people vs. the impacted is how a person decides to spend their time.

So, let me ask you. How are you spending your time?

Are the so-called teenage "norms" consuming your time?

Is it a boy or girl?

Hours of video games?

TikTok?

Drinking?
Netflix?
Or porn?

If the world can rob you of your time as a teen, it will make you miss doors that might be standing wide open for you.

If you took just thirty minutes every day, which is only three and a half hours out of one 168 hours a week, you could write a book, transform your physique, or start a YouTube channel.

In this day and age, your options are endless. You have to start and be intentional. It's time to stand out. It's to become the influencer.

Listen. I've already said it. You have the same time as everyone else. What are you doing to do with it?

We all have been blessed with the same twenty-four hours in a day. It's up to you to decide how you will spend it.

It is said that the average teen spends seven-plus hours a day on screen time, and that does not include schoolwork.

"So what?" you may ask. "Everyone else is doing it. It is just how our society works."

Okay, you can use that excuse to justify a lot of things, *especially* sins.

But you *aren't* just anybody. You are here to make a difference.

Don't worry about making excuses to people who aren't supporting you.

Hanging out with people content with staying at the bottom will not get you to the top.

So, *I dare you* to stand out.

I dare you to stand up.

Be different.

Use your time to create an impact on the lives around you.

Stop letting everyone else affect your emotions, your day, your life.

You choose your life, friends, and mood.

You possess the power to choose the direction of your life.

No one else can.

It is time for you to *lock in* and get focused.

Everyone is unique, so this will look different for everyone. Perhaps your focus point is your grades because you want to become a doctor. Or maybe you want to become the next world record-breaking Olympic gold medalist.

You are going to have to carve out the time, the dedication, and the consistency needed to get there. That might mean deleting TikTok and devoting that extra time to an extra hour of sleep, or it could mean waking up an hour earlier so you can write a chapter in your next book.

Whatever getting focused looks like for you, it's time for you to zone in and give yourself to it 110 percent.

Because how are you going to be *somebody* if you are acting like *everybody*?

CHARACTERISTIC SIX

VALUE

> For every minute the future is becoming the past.
> —Thor Heyerdahl

Relationships are crucial when it comes to building up who you are. When you look around, especially post-pandemic of 2020, we as people have separated ourselves from having relationships. Closing ourselves off from what life used to be like.

This reality has been a challenge. I love spending time with people, but I also adore my alone time. However, closing your door and never coming out is not the answer. Yes, for a time, we were forced to shut every door and window to the outside world. But it is time to come back out. It's time to dance and to laugh!

Friendships

Going back to school after quarantine was really strange. We had to "socially" distance. People were silent. Students didn't talk in class, and it was really hard to make new friends because you couldn't get near anybody without risking making them uncomfortable, not knowing if they were ok if you stepped within six feet.

This was and still is a mental game. In my opinion, the term "socially distant" is incorrect. We technically should be calling it "physically distant."

Why can't we still make friends, talk, and be with each other at a time like this?

In fact, more than ever, we need people to relate to and talk to because, in a world full of people, there are millions who feel alone.

Wake up from that lie. You are not alone.

I know it can be so easy to fake a smile and hide your pain. As the world becomes more digital, it's going to be even easier. I encourage you, however, to be authentic. Someone else is hurting too, and they understand what you are facing.

As teens, we focus so much on friendships. Our entire world can feel as if it is falling apart if we lose someone we once trusted or if we just can't seem to fit in with the popular crowd.

I have found that life runs smoother when you have a few close friends compared to fourteen peers you just hang with but never talk with. From my experience, I have found that building a friendship takes time and experience. There truly is a difference when your friend becomes a best friend.

What's the difference between a friend and a best friend?

Well, a friend is going to love you and have fun with you.

A best friend loves you, will die for you, cry with you, and will tell you when you are in the wrong. They are the rare friends who can call at any time, and the two of you can talk for hours, never realizing a second has ticked by.

A good identifier in a best friend is the two of you do not drain each other's social batteries. As best friends, you understand what the other person needs to recharge.

You are also able to recognize when your friend is struggling or needs a break in a social environment.

You look out for each other.

You can rant and then offer advice.

You can talk or not talk.

It's all about being able to have a healthy balanced relationship that's fun and essential to your personal growth at the same time. A true friend is a person you can trust and tell everything to. This person is a best friend.

Some of my past friends and I were only close for a time. We made great memories, but not everything is meant to last. When I moved, I thought nothing would change with some of my old friends. At some point, however, I began to feel distant, left out, and alone.

I feared our friendships were over.

And a lot of them did end. Most of those people I no longer talk to.

When you change, whether that is your location, your mentality, or your beliefs, people are going to leave.

I cannot tell you the number of friendships that have closed in my life from the time I was in seventh grade to twelfth grade.

People change, and you have to decide whether to change with them or part ways. Sometimes people leave you, and sometimes you need to go.

Not all close friendships are healthy. You may not notice at first, but certain people can weave their way into your life or your friends' lives, slowly changing you or someone you know. You must be wise about whom you spend your time with because they will influence who you will become.

I am going to be straight with you.

When you know who you are and what direction you are heading, people will dislike you. They will be jealous, and they will want to destroy your passion. Do not let their Jezebel spirit push you off your path. You have the right to choose who gets your attention and who receives your love.

Pray for everyone, some more than others. You don't have to be friends with everyone. Some people are toxic and will claim control over your life. They will make you feel exhausted, frustrated, and empty.

You have to know when to "drop" a friend or create distance with people. It is a tool I have learned to use a lot in high school.

Now, you don't blow up and just leave the big group chat on iMessage or unfollow them on the 'Gram. Be wise. Do it slowly and delicately. You do not want your reputation being damaged by this person because they feel offended in some way.

For me, I slowly stopped sitting with specific people at lunch and in class. I stopped texting them over time. And I stopped letting them get in my head.

In other words, I did not worry about them. Their choices were not mine. I cannot control them or take the blame for them. All I can do is pray and be there for them at a distance.

People will make their choices, and you will have to make yours. Sometimes you just have to know when to establish a boundary and let them decide whether they want to change or not.

A good friendship takes time, just as bad relationships can take time to reveal themselves. You have to be mindful and listen to the people who love you; they will usually spot bad relationships miles before you can.

You have to remember that some people are impatient and selfish. They are not going to think about what is best for you or whether or not you might enjoy something. Friends are going to fail, hurt, and disappoint you because they are human—especially if they are not a child of God.

Do not look to fill yourself up from people because God is the only one who can do that. You cannot align your identity with the fact that people do not want to hang around you or that you don't seem to fit it.

You are different.

You were not meant to hide away in the sea of the unknown.

I say all this to remind you not to close away your heart but to protect it. You have to build a foundation of trust and show an amount of vulnerability when letting someone into your life. You may go through a dry season of friendships, but then the rain falls, and someone sent from God will come into your life.

Trust me; it is worth the wait. I never would take back any of my old relationships because they not only taught me how to be a friend but also, they set the path that led me to my best friends.

I believe that to grow in friendship, you have to commit to spending quality time with that friend. It doesn't matter if you live miles away. We can connect in seconds. Send them a text or start a weekly Facetime. No, it's not the same as an in-person connection, nor is it ideal. Yet, you're sowing seeds in the relationship.

Even if this friend is in your life for a moment, make it your goal to leave a lasting impact on their life.

How can you serve them?

For me, going to lunch with someone is a good way to show them you care enough to spend time with them outside your crazy everyday life. Or bringing them something they love, like Milo's Sweet Tea or a Monster Energy Drink, will show you were thinking about them.

I challenge you to look at your friendships.

Are they building you up or tearing you down?

Is it a one-way or a two-way relationship?

Is it really bringing you joy?

God will show you who needs to be in your life. Be intentional by looking for the signs he gives you and the doors he has open for you.

Boyfriend/Girlfriend

Ok, now for a subject that seems to take up a lot of our time and thoughts as teens.

Dating. Boys. Girls.
Listen up, girls.
Life does not revolve around guys.
Listen up, guys.
Life does not revolve around girls.

There is so much more than how many times you've gone on a date or if he looked your way. If you use your time in high school to focus on discovering who you are as a person and who you are in the Lord, then you don't have to worry about gaining attention from boys or girls.

So what if you haven't had your first kiss?
So what if you haven't gone on a date?
There will be a time when you will find *the* one.

Sleeping around with one boy or girl one day and drooling over another the next day is not the way. Engaging in these patterns devalues you and the relationship. That is not how you make stable, lifetime relationships. These actions could ruin your reputation and your life. You have to learn how to have balance, priorities, and boundaries before you step into an intimate relationship.

When should you start dating?
Determining a time can be complicated. Your parents' authority is important, and if they say you can't date until you are sixteen, seventeen, or eighteen, then you need to listen to them. However, if it is up to you, be wise.

Being obsessed with guys or girls may not be a problem for you. But if you are obsessed with boys or girls and worship the idea of having a boyfriend or girlfriend instead of worshipping the one who created you, then there is a problem.

There are also sins or baggage that you may need to overcome before stepping into a relationship, such as porn or sexual sins and addictions. If you don't overcome these hardships, you are not only going to be extremely tempted, but you will hurt the person you are dating, with the possibility of affecting their lives for years to come.

Let's get real; at the beginning of high school, none of us are ready for a relationship. There is a lot of identity development that occurs during your freshman and sophomore years.

Even if you are an upperclassman and you are dating, you should not be posting photos online of you kissing and hugging at the age of seventeen. You are too young to open your heart to that kind of love. There is so much more life and time ahead of you. And if you really have found the one, remember that love is patient, and when it's time, God will let you know.

Of course, dating in high school when you are seventeen or eighteen is a different conversation than at fourteen, fifteen, or sixteen.

Yet again, when you are a senior, there are still so many questions that are still unanswered. For example, are you going to go to the same college or are you going to try long-distance?

Relationships take a lot of your time. Even when you aren't with them, you'll find yourself thinking about them, and you can become distracted very easily. Love songs, writings, movies, etc., all start meaning something more.

Before you open your heart to love, dive deep into learning more about yourself because if you know who you are, you won't lose yourself in someone else. And if you know who you are in God, you will not enter an ungodly relationship.

Relationships can bring up many insecurities and uncertainties because of the broken world we live in. Many people fear commitment, lack healthy communication skills, and the idea of a good marriage crumbles.

A lot of times, people go into relationships expecting things or needing things that only God can provide. When this happens, all the baggage and hurt from both people can cause a toxic relationship to be born.

We must be aware of wrong expectations when it comes to relationships. Love is not found in a Hollywood movie. Love involves both hard and good times.

Misconceptions are being fed to us from adults who have been hurt in the past, from the movies we watch, etc. Divorce rates are at an all-time high because our culture has taught us to keep a way out in our back pocket. Love requires a covenant that isn't easily broken.

People are falling in and out of love because they are not learning how to love unconditionally. That is how God loves, and it is something we should all strive for. Because, unlike the movies, soulmates aren't found; they are made.

Two people loving each other is a beautiful thing. God designed people to *become one* through the covenant of marriage. A healthy relationship between a man and woman looks like a triangle. God at the top and husband/wife or boyfriend/girlfriend at the bottom points. If you move closer to God, you will naturally move closer together.

As teens, most of us aren't ready for marriage, but we can start learning what we want our future relationship to be like.

Whether you are dating or single, learning about what you want your future relationship to look like or become is important. One thing that has been helpful for me is reading books such as *Single, Dating, Engaged, Married* by Ben Stuart, or *Outdated* by Jonathan "JP" Pokluda. These books offered different ideas and advice that will help as you prepare for your future spouse and family.

If you are dating, talk with your boyfriend or girlfriend about important and critical topics that affect your relationship. And please, if you are just dating for "fun," consider reevaluating why you need or are in this relationship. If it is an unhealthy relationship and you cannot end it on your own, do not hesitate to get help from a trusted adult.

Some example topics would be what boundaries will you want to develop, do you want to have daily devotionals, how can you be committed to church together, etc.

Another thing you can do, single or not, is find a couple that you can strive to be like. This could be someone like Sadie Robertson and Christian Huff, or maybe it's your grandparents or your parents. It could be anyone, but remember, no one is perfect.

Relationships are complicated when it comes to family and friends, but a relationship that could lead to a friend becoming family—that's intimidating yet exciting. As long as you keep the Lord first and listen to his instructions, then you will find the one.

Now a note to the boyfriends and girlfriends.

When you are dating, I believe character is one of the most important things in a relationship. You also should be on the same page when it comes to God and His Kingdom.

Remember that beauty fades. You are not guaranteed anything in life. Tomorrow you could be in a burn accident, or you could, unfortunately, get really sick. That is the crazy, unexpected way of life. However, you can always choose your attitude and focus. What is on the inside is what truly matters. And you can see how a person is on the inside by the way a person acts around you, their friends, and their family.

Boyfriends, never stop respecting and showing your love to your girlfriend. Surprise her with flowers, plan a date to watch the sunset, send her a text while she sleeps that she can awake to, open the door for her, make sure she's okay, listen to her, ask her questions about topics that interest her, put your phone down and just be with her, etc.

Girlfriends, never stop respecting and showing your love to your boyfriend. Send him texts throughout the day, pray for him, bring him his favorite food, learn the language of his favorite sport, spend time with his siblings, learn to listen, be able to sit and watch him play his videogames, etc.

We all show love differently, whether that is physical touch, words of affirmation, quality time, acts of service, or receiving gifts.

Dating allows us how to learn those different languages through expressing love in a healthy and safe environment.

You are going to have to sacrifice, learn, and grow in a relationship. Dating is complicated, and it is especially important to have a strong community around you that makes sure that you are not being tempted to fall off the path God has for you.

This community can be trusted adults, parents, church family, other Christian couples your age, etc. They are there to encourage and give you advice and wisdom. This support group is important because our feelings for someone can skew healthy perspectives.

Dating someone when you are young will impact and shape the person you will become.

If you are dating someone in an evaluation mindset, your end goal should be marriage. When dating, you should be helping your girlfriend or boyfriend become not only closer to God but also a better spouse for their future spouse (whether that's you or not).

The best thing is if you both understand that you are not the one who God has for you, you both can walk away knowing you became a stronger and better person because of the relationship. It will eliminate a lot of hurt. Nevertheless, you will probably still get hurt, but it won't leave an open wound.

And the most amazing, sacred, and rare part is when God shows you the person you are meant to be with. It is a miraculous moment when you realize the person you have been helping grow will get to be part of your life for many years to come. You get to spend the rest of your life doing work for God's Kingdom with this amazing person who has come into your life at the right time and place.

Siblings

What is different between a sibling and a best friend?

Difference number one—we tend to fight a bit more.

We know how to push every single button and when to push them to make each other explode. It's all fun and games until someone's feelings are hurt, and it leads to hurt. Now, we all are in trouble.

Even when I pick on my sisters or they call me a peasant, I still love my sisters. They make me a better person. Even when I don't want to hear the good, the bad, and the ugly about myself or what I am doing, they let me know.

A sibling relationship is complicated; we hate it when we have to share clothes, but we would jump in front of a bus to save each other's lives.

When I am hurting, my sisters are always there to either a) comfort me, b) prepare to take out whoever hurt me, and c) or make fun of me until I laugh.

Daily, I work to be a better sister because I know I mess up. I say things that weren't meant to be said, or I fail to spend more time with my sisters and brother.

I believe a sister is honest, loyal, and trustworthy. A sister is there in times of need and celebration. Even from afar, the simplest act of a sister can completely rewrite one's current state of emotion. A true sister will always desire to be a better sister.

Now, I don't know about you, but my youngest sibling is an angel—unless he teams up with one of my other sisters. Then he is their little minion to be used as they wish.

I am kidding. I love my little brother. He is goofy and always knows how to make one of us girls laugh.

My brother is completely different from all the girls in my family. He is carefree and just loves to enjoy life. He is always going to be the first one to get me a glass of water or ask me if I am alright. I love him so much.

Once again, intentionality is key when it comes to a relationship. We have to be intentional about spending time with those we love. For my siblings and I, we do a couple of the following things:

- We watch a show together.
- My sister, Aliyah, and I are huge *Gilmore Girls* fans (currently waiting for another spinoff, please, and thank you @netflix). The bond we have over those shows will never end because we have laughed, cried, and been angry at characters together. We have most likely spent an unhealthy number of hours watching *Gilmore Girls* to the point where we know what is going to happen in every episode, especially those with Jess Mariano in them (we are both Jess Mariano lovers, and forever we shall be).
- Fooooood.
- Food is one of the best ways to bond with people. When my sisters have something to tell me, whether it's boy-related or schoolgirl fanatic, we usually head to grab a smoothie or sandwich and just talk. Even

if it's less than an hour, those precious moments are worth more than a million dollars.

- Music
- All three of my sisters and I have completely different tastes in music. We literally have less than a ten percent blend mix score on Spotify.

How can three people in one house be so different?

My younger sister, Makena, has the most different music taste from me. When I am taking her to school in the morning, we've had to be intentional about creating a playlist with music we both like.

At first, it was a struggle.

Neither of us wanted to cave when it came to choosing a song. However, now we both have stretched our love for types of music. Because even if I kind of hate ninety-nine percent of her music, I am usually introduced to a song that I would add to my playlist (this is such a rare moment, but I am sure she feels the same).

Once we started sharing the air with our music, we started to get to know each other better.

And that allows us to bond, even if it means laughing at the fact that we go from Why Don't We Love Songs to popping Michael Jackson tunes as we jam through the night sky with the windows rolled down and the volume on max.

- Bike rides.
- My brother and I, if given the choice, would bike 24/7. It's a way both of us can be competitive and have fun at the same time. If we were playing another sport, my brother would not ask me to play because I dominate (I am slightly competitive).

Biking, however, is different. I just love to ride, but he loves the race, so it evens the playing ground.

Some of my favorite nights are when he "spills the tea" on sixth-grade drama. I literally have no idea who he is talking about, but take my word for it; you don't want to mess with those boy-crazy girls in sixth grade. They are mean.

In the end, there are an unlimited number of ways to spend time with your sibling. And I am not going to lie, there are days that I want to slap my siblings across the face, but that would not be the right thing to do.

Plus, I would reap a good grounding.

Allow the right amount of time, space, and patience when you feel angry or frustrated with your sister or brother. And remember, you guys are different in almost every way, age, struggles, and the way you mentally process things.

To all my readers who are older siblings like me, your siblings are watching you. They admire you. Yes, they love you even if they crash into your room daily, knocking all your decor off the wall.

They want to be with you, and they are struggling with similar stuff you once did. Take the time to listen to them and allow them into your space occasionally. The best thing you can do for them is give them a chance to speak their opinions. Even if it doesn't make total sense, allowing them the chance to be seen is key to letting them feel loved.

To all the younger siblings, your older siblings love you. Just remember, they are heading into adulthood first. They are facing struggles you will one day face too.

You don't always have to keep asking us why we are upset because sometimes we don't even know what we are feeling. It might be because, deep down, we are sad or anxious that we are leaving soon.

We can feel life changing and a new and unknown season approaching fast. One that you are not in 24/7. The best thing you can do to help us, is remind us to have fun and not stress so much. You are a reflection of our inner child.

If your relationship with your siblings is in bad shape right now, take the first step to start the process of healing. A first step may simply be saying, "I am sorry." Most of the time, we aren't angry with our siblings, but we are frustrated with school, parents, friends, or life in general. We tend to take it out on our siblings because we know that they will always be there—until they aren't.

Don't let time fade away to a point when you wake up, and the closest friends you could have had are gone.

Parents

Parents are a complex conversation.

Every person has a different feeling that erupts inside when one brings up this topic. Our parents are supposed to be there for us from the time we are born to when we are on our own.

The idea of being a parent is intimidating because the parents' actions, opinions, emotions, environment, etc., shape a child's world. If a parent is not in a child's life or fails to live up to their duties as a mother or father, it impacts the child for a lifetime.

Things built up from the loss of a parent, the absence of a parent, a bad relationship with a parent, etc., create difficult struggles that we need to overcome as teens and then, later on, when we become parents ourselves.

Most parent issues are pushed upon the teen, even when it is not their fault. This is not fair, but that is life. Plus, your story is being shaped, and that story has the power to help someone else through a similar situation.

Why should you find that encouraging?

Because you may well be the only person who can help someone else through what they are feeling and struggling with, you will be able to understand them unlike anybody else because you faced that storm already.

Some kids grow up with parents who try their hardest, while others grow up being the parent because their mom or dad lives in brokenness. It can be easy to see our parents as perfect when we are younger and then be totally shocked when you find out they aren't.

Our parents have dreams that never came true. They have goals they want to achieve. They have been hurt and haven't healed. They were teenagers too. They have bad and good days.

You can't blame yourself for your parents' mistakes and actions. Yes, respect them and honor them no matter the situation. You have to set boundaries. Don't let their disrespect define you. Understand that they are your authority. When you understand your parents aren't flawless, you can give them the grace to make mistakes. They are not a perfect representation of who God is.

Do they reflect him?

Yes, for example, God gives us rules to protect us. Parents do the same.

Why are we told not to play with fire?

Because it burns.

When we don't listen, we get hurt.

Parents will say and do things that hurt you, but you cannot let your relationship with your parents hinder your relationship with God. Your parents are not God. Don't blame Him for their actions.

God lets you face things that will challenge you but not crush you. You will never face anything you cannot overcome because Christ has already conquered.

If you are struggling with your relationship with your parents, I recommend finding the right place and time to talk with them.

Let them know how you are feeling. Be honest but speak with wisdom. Make sure you have this conversation when no one is heated because there can be a lot of miscommunications when your emotions are charged. Think first, then speak. Some conversations with parent(s) may need to be with a counselor.

Not everybody can or is willing to change, and you certainly cannot make them change. Remember that sometimes, after it seems like we have tried everything, the best we can do for someone is pray for God to work in their lives.

CHARACTERISTIC SEVEN

WISDOM

**The problem is not the problem.
The problem is your attitude about the problem.**

—Jack Sparrow (*Pirates of the Caribbean*)

When we were kids, people would ask us, "What do you want to be when you grow up?"

We would reply with such clarity and passion. I was sure that I was going to be the next Disney Channel star! I admired Zendaya, Dove, Selena, and Miley. I wanted to be doing what they were doing. Well, I wanted to be living their polished life. I had no idea what they were really facing behind the curtains.

When I was in second grade, I actually auditioned to be on *Shake It Up*. There was a competition going on called Make Your Mark. I ended up making it to the second round, where I dressed up in a rock star outfit inspired by Rocky. I filmed my audition on my church's stage with lights, cameras, and *confetti*!

It was so much fun, but I didn't get a callback for the in-person audition.

Did I care?

A little.

But I moved on to my next focus, which was probably reading the next *Nancy Drew* book or basketball.

Flash forward to today; I am glad I did not get a callback. Who knows where or who I would be if I had won.

There is so much about Hollywood that was unknown to the world and has begun to come out. I don't know if I would have wanted to sacrifice my childhood so soon to a world that would have used me for their own selfish benefit. It breaks my heart for all the kids in Hollywood who grow up too fast and even have lost their lives to some of the greatest sins.

Kids are growing up too fast because of exposure to TV programs and movies developed by the sinisters in Hollywood. It happens every day.

Slowly, if we are not careful, we are being exposed to "sins" that mankind wants to normalize—pornography, casual sex, child abuse, drugs, racism, homosexuality. Every day, we are challenged by this reality that someone who has an agenda has created.

In order to normalize these sins, they place them in commercials, in our movies, shows, music videos, in the lyrics of music, makeup campaigns, the pushed, scripted, and biased news media, our school history books—the list is endless.

It's not surprising why so many of us teens are struggling with our identity because these outright sins are not attacking us physically but rather mentally. They are fighting to shape our mindset. The world is pressing in.

What we let in through our minds goes into our hearts. What is entering our hearts can make us bitter and cause us to develop thoughts we never knew we could think. It's a trap that leads us to hate not just ourselves but the people around us.

Jealousy, hatred, confusion—it all begins to consume us.

This assault causes us to separate ourselves voluntarily from each other. We start to think the worst of people because they support the opposite political party, were born in another country, have a different skin color than you, or have grown up in a family unlike yours.

You will miss out on so many opportunities to impact the world if you stay locked inside your own safe bubble. You have to use wisdom with what you watch and consume daily because that is how your mentality is shaped.

It's a sad and shocking realization, but most people don't even realize the judgmental, racist, accusing beliefs they have grown up believing.

If you think of a street gang, what type of person comes to your mind?

If you think of "organized crime," what type of person comes to your mind?

Note that those are terms the media uses daily to make you think that one is less destructive than the other.

But, in reality, both kill, steal, and destroy. A lie seems innocent until you start to live it.

Listen, you might need to turn off the news. When you allow it into your life, it will influence you. It is not wise to be consuming it 24/7. Yes, be aware of today's events, but get your resources from more than just the news on your local channel.

Research for yourself. An influencer becomes educated with the facts for themselves. Don't let someone on the screen tell you their *scripted* opinion or "fact."

How do you know it's true?

Who is telling the story?

What perspective are they coming from?

Find a way to get past the labels the world puts on us, or you will never be able to reach your purpose.

Life isn't all about you.

The world isn't revolving around me. Your purpose is bigger than you.

But there are issues and things that can be changed if we come together in wisdom and intentionality. We are searching for who we are. We are trying to overcome something. Stop judging each other and take time to get to know someone else. Ask them about their dreams and empower them. Finding clarity of what your dream is in life can be difficult but supporting each other helps us get there.

As I write this, I am struggling to figure out who I am supposed to become and who I am supposed to help in life. There are so many paths to take (and tunnels to escape). It can be outright overwhelming to decide which path to take next. Sometimes we can talk ourselves out of things because we fear the unknown.

I literally did this while I was writing this book.

I have felt unqualified because I'm going through things as a teen right now that I have not overcome. I am currently struggling with stuff that I've written about in this book. I don't always follow my own advice. I make mistakes and change my mind. I get off track and waste time. Should I quit? Am I disqualified?

No, I choose to stand back up. I always keep fighting for what I believe in and for whom I love. I choose to stand out in a world pressing in.

It's so easy to be afraid of success or failure. The freeing reality is that I have a choice. You have a choice.

To find clarity about where you are going, just start somewhere. Stop obsessing over others, stop wasting your time, and become willing to fail, to wait, to turn the wrong way, to lean on others, and to hold others up. Taking steps of faith is how we learn. Doing new things gives you the opportunity to find out if that is for you or not.

Notice I did not say try. As Yoda says, "Do or do not. There is no try."

When you try things, you are allowing yourself a loophole to get out early. You have to commit and challenge yourself with a task to see if you love it or not.

• • •

You wake up and decide, "Hey, I am going to start working out today."

So, you run a mile for the first time, and you bike for twenty minutes. The whole time, you feel like you might die.

Sweat is dripping off you, your heart is racing, and your mind is screaming, "*Brooooo*. What are you doing to me?"

The next day, you are thinking, well, that sucked. I don't think working out is for me.

First off, you are not going to know what it feels like to make progress if you stop before you even make any progress.

Second, if that workout didn't connect with you, do another one. Yesterday's workout was only one type of workout. There are an endless number of workouts out there. All are different in action, specialize in different areas, have different results, different variations, different tools, different skill sets, and different levels of intensity.

But when you combine different types of workouts, you can achieve maximum results in a more effective amount of time. It's almost like with people. Wisdom is gained through consistent action.

CHARACTERISTIC EIGHT

PATIENCE

Successful people do what others know they should do but will not.

—Chalene Johnson

Patience.
What is patience?
Nowadays, we have so little experience when it comes to waiting for things to happen.
We can get our grades instantly after taking an online test, while our parents had to wait for their grades to be graded by a human being and then posted on a wall.
We can heat up food in seconds, while our grandparents slaved in the kitchen for hours and sometimes days in advance to prepare one meal.
We can order groceries and have them delivered to our home within hours, while our grandparents had to wait through the seasons to have crops ready for consumption.
We can text our friends, and in seconds we have an answer or satisfaction from their reply, while our parents and grandparents had to either send letters, page someone and, if

they had a house phone, there was a time limit, and someone else in the neighborhood could easily listen in.

Life is so much different nowadays than it was years ago.

We live in a world where patience seems to be unnecessary until we must implement it. The only problem is that we have not been trained on what it takes or what it means to be patient.

Where we are going and what we will be doing can seem intimidating or out of reach.

We long to be finished with college, have a job, travel the world, or have a family.

Or some of us avoid thinking about the future. It can be frustrating when you are stuck in life because the season you are in has not ended.

Personally, I catch myself thinking about what my life is going to be like in less than a year.

Will I be in college?

Or traveling afar?

What will my relationship with my family be like?

This is normal.

It's going to be so strange going from being quarantined with a family of six and three dogs to living in a dorm with people I either have never met or have known only for a short while.

Now, I can't wait till I get to the "living in my own apartment" phase of my life. I want to decorate my home, cook my own meals, buy cute utensils, set up my own little workout area, etc. However, though that is all so exciting, I know that without the patience and hard work in the present, I will never make it to that future.

We have to learn to wait. If you were to jump at every opportunity that opens up for you, you would never get anywhere.

You might be thinking, *well, thanks for the inspiring speech that my parents have already told me. I know I am impatient, but that's just how I am. I can't change.*

You can change, and you are changing. The power to change, however, is unlocked when you are intentional about the change.

Here are some key factors that will allow you to learn to wait. I call it the *P3*.

1. Pause. Relax.

A lot of the time, with impatience, comes anxiety. For example, I was trying to figure out what I was supposed to do this year as a senior. There were a lot of doors opened before me, which caused a tornado to crash throughout my brain.

So many different scenarios.

So many different outcomes.

Yet, each time I stepped up to a door, a slamming sound echoed before me. I felt lost and confused, and there were some tears of frustration that left my eyes.

Finally, there was one door that I hoped would open for me. It made total sense. Anticipation filled my body. I woke up every day for a week wondering if just maybe I'd know the answer.

Yet, I was turned away, and another door proved to be tightly locked.

Disappointment, confusion, and frustration crushed me. It still weighs on my heart thinking about it because it is something that I had wanted for a long time, but even after trying to have patience and faith, it didn't fall into place. So, I had to go back to being patient and waiting for God to move. Patience is hard, but in the end, it will all be worth it.

Being a senior in high school can be one of the hardest seasons. You are in between your past and your future; child and adult; school and career. You're preparing for your next while still living in the now.

We have to learn patience, or life will make us anxious, stressed, and unhappy. Pause and know that God is ultimately going to work everything out for the good if you give it to him.

2. Perceive. Be mindful of the things making you impatient.

- It can feel as if every second we have an alarm going off, an alert from Instagram, a new Tik Tok was just posted, a grade posted by our teacher, or our favorite YouTuber just dropped a new video.

Everything is fighting for our attention, and a lot of times, we let the phone win the battle.

Our phones can become escapes and distractions from the chaos of our lives. I know when I am having a bad day, it can be really tempting to just swipe through Instagram, which only makes things worse because I start to compare myself to others.

The distractions caused by our phones actually support a life of impatience. Our mind becomes trained to receive instantaneous alerts. Distracted living is not healthy for you.

Make a decision to turn off the alerts. Recognize which alerts you need and which are unnecessary.

Mute those group chats.

Silence your DMs and post notifications.

After a week, your mind is going to feel much more at peace.

It might be, and most likely will be, challenging at first because phones are addicting. We pick up our phones expecting that there will be people reaching out to us and when there isn't, a lonely feeling can settle into our stomachs.

It might take breaking away from your phone a little while for you to see the true beauty of patience.

3. Be Patient. Practice **Patience**. Develop a discipline of waiting.
- If you learn to practice patience with the little things, waiting for the large things will become easier and less consuming. Start with waiting ten minutes after you get hungry to make your food. Then try waiting three days before you watch the next episode of your favorite show. Keep building and experimenting with your patience.

Put the *P3* to work for you. 1. Pause, 2. perceive, and 3. practice patience.

CHARACTERISTIC NINE

ADAPTABILITY

I want adventure in the great wide somewhere!
I want it more than I can tell!

—**Belle (***Beauty and The Beast)*

The amount of time you have on Earth is unknown by all but the Maker.

In life, it is important to have plans and goals. When you wake up, you should have a to-do list that maps out what you want to get done in the day. Learning to have three focus points in a day is a game-changer. You should have a purpose to make the most of your day.

Teenfluencers create a networked spontaneous plan for your life.

Flexibility.

Flow. Intentionality. Purpose. Accomplishment.

What is a networked spontaneous plan?

Let's break it down by starting with the definitions.

Definitions.

Network: a group or system of interconnected people or things.

Spontaneous: performed or occurring because of a sudden inner impulse or inclination and without premeditation or external stimulus.

Plan: a detailed proposal for doing or achieving something.

You might be thinking, how can I have a plan and be spontaneous at the same time, and what in the world does a network have anything to do with any of this?

Let's start with network since it's first on the list.

Our life is a network of activity, people, and moving parts. The actions we make impact the work of others.

When you live out of your purpose, all that you do starts to line up. Your goals and dreams become centered in who you are meant to be. Every action you take has intentionality attached to it. Everything starts working together and is intertwined even if it does not look like it. From within, you know everything you do is networking toward your future. Even failure is connected to your success.

You get to decide if failure is failure or if it is the next step to your success. Next, we have to be spontaneous. With so many things to do and so many people heading in different directions and having unexpected interruptions, there is no possible way for one day to look the same as the last.

You are going to have setbacks and sometimes a complete turn of events. If you are not careful, you can end up wasting your time if you dwell on the fact that nothing is going according to your plan.

In the not-so-distant past, I would get really stressed out when the plan did not go according to my plan. I felt so out of control because every year, it was like my life got flipped upside down. I had no way to prepare for what was next, and even when I did, something would always change.

Life in a big family never seems to go as planned. I really struggled with this battle until this year, when everything, once again, decided to change.

The usual plan for high school seniors of going to a traditional school was not my path. I gained new friends who were truly sent from God who lived six hours from me, except for one who just *had* to live across the United States. Cough, cough.

My family was putting our house on the market because God was directing us even when we had no clue where we would be moving. I decided that one of my next assignments was to invest in these new relationships truly centered in Christ, even if that meant spending money on gas and time. Because to me, connections and memories are so much more valuable than getting the most college credits possible.

I will never get this time back.

At the same time as all this was happening, my car decided to break down. This setback meant we had to make a new plan. It's a crazy story, and the story is still unfolding. Stay tuned! Maybe I will share the rest of the story in my next book.

The reason I am able to live such a spontaneous life is because of three things.

1. **I have faith and a God-given peace that is from my Savior, Jesus Christ.** Wherever he sends me, I go. It is not going to look traditional. I mean, look at me now. I am sitting in a cafe writing my second book when most teens are sitting in a classroom (which is all amazing, I am definitely not the one studying to be a doctor. I want you to see that life does not have to be traditional for you to be successful).

2. **I adapt.** When you have a goal, you must adapt to your surroundings and the events occurring around you.

For example, if you are working on your physical appearance, you have this goal to gain fifteen pounds, but suddenly you have to start traveling more.

What do you do?

How are you supposed to eat healthy when you are on the road?

Well, first, it is about balance.

You may not be able to eat clean all the time, but plan to eat healthy when the option is available. If you don't have a plan, you will be influenced and not the influencer. Did you bring some protein bars in case you need a healthy snack?

And what about the gym?

You are most likely going to have to make an investment in a national gym membership in hotels that have a gym or travel equipment.

There is always a way, and yes, it might be inconvenient. But when you push through, the reward is going to be so much greater. Trust me.

Number three blends into our last definition.

Plan. Without a plan, you will not achieve your goals. As Benjamin Franklin said, "If you fail to plan, you are planning to fail."

It's that simple.

And without a good plan, you are not going to achieve your goals effectively or efficiently.

3. **I have long-term plans supported by mini-plans.**
   When you are living in a world run on a network, and you have to be spontaneous to keep up with life. It is important to have a plan with daily goals.

   You do not need each second planned out because you have to leave room for spontaneity, yet you should also have a list of what you need to get done. Every day should bring you one step closer to your future aim.

My tip for you is to have three things you plan to do each day. For example

- Read the Bible first thing in the morning,
- Workout for one hour,
- Write 1,000 words in your next book.

After that, you might have to go to school, study math, or learn Chinese.

Who knows?

All our schedules will look different, but if you focus on three top things consistently every day—over time—you will make exponential progress. Some days we might be pushed backward; others, we might take five leaps forward. The key is to keep moving forward.

One more tip that will lead you to living a networked spontaneous planned life is implementing flexibility. Getting a job that allows you to work flexible hours allows you time to invest in your passion *unless* that certain job is your passion.

Yes, we've got to work to make money to fund our passions. And, at first, our passions are not going to produce the income we hope for. However, flexibility brings time, and time brings money.

So, jump on the ride of life. Plan to buckle your seat belt and throw your hands in the air because you are not going to be heading uphill all your life. There will be loops, turns, and drops.

The question is, are you going to hold on tight, terrified over what's next, or open your eyes and enjoy the ride?

CHARACTERISTIC TEN

CONNECTION

> Anyone who waits for someone else to make a change automatically becomes a follower.
> —Peyton Manning

Life is not fair.

You can bust your butt serving other people—waking up before sunrise to pick up breakfast for your team, filling in when others don't show, or redesigning the system so it flows better—but sometimes outcomes are out of your control.

It happens all the time in Hollywood. An actor can go in and rock an audition, and the casting directors can love them, but the movie director wants his friend, or someone with a well-known name, to star so that person gets the part instead. The other person just gets a 'better luck next time.'

Not getting the part, losing class president, or not getting into a dream school are all results that happen even when you do everything right, but oftentimes one person has the power to stop that dream.

I challenge you to step back and reflect on a different perspective.

Maybe it's God protecting you. Maybe God has something better for you.

Who knows?

Sometimes we will never understand the whys until years later. We don't always have an answer to why good people get turned away. But we have to keep our focus. We have to keep our intentions pure and follow where God is directing us.

In life, it is important to build connections because you never know who might open a door in your life next. Connections come with time, dedication, and intention.

When you walk into a room, don't hide in a corner. No, you do not need to talk to everybody; just talk to somebody. Walk up to someone new and try to get to know them.

How?

Ask them questions about their passions, dreams, and aspirations.

For instance, what's your dream place to travel or what's something you want to learn to do this year? Planning can work here also. Instead of asking, "well, isn't the sky blue today?" prepare questions in advance. Practice asking them in the mirror if that helps. Plan to meet people. You never know when that person might have the key to open the door to your next best step.

Listening is key when it comes to creating connections because most people feel unheard. When you take the time to let someone speak, they feel honored, and in return, most of the time, they will honor you back, and the door for you to share has opened.

Another key factor that listening allows you to do is to find what motivates them. What makes them tick? Is this a person you might want to invest time in?

Perhaps you could learn from them, or they could learn from you?

If not, don't pursue a relationship. It was just a connection. Nevertheless, while you are with this person, be kind and wise to build up your reputation. You never know what purpose the connection will serve. Perhaps, you will help them, or they will help you.

One tip that I have used when building connections is to listen to people in a way where you catch things that they say they enjoy, like, or want, and you file them away in your memory. That way, when they are least expecting it, you show them a token of appreciation. For example, maybe someone's favorite dessert is banana pudding, so you don't just buy them a cup of banana pudding. No, you (or your mom) make them homemade banana pudding that could feed their family on Thanksgiving.

This not only shows them that you listen but that you cared enough to think about them so that you took action to show it. It shows intention and dedication. It allows someone to trust you. And every time they see banana pudding, it will remind them that somewhere out there, someone sees them and is willing to serve them with intentionality.

Connections are going to open doors in your life, and the connections that people have with you will open doors in your life.

Gifts open hearts, and open hearts open doors.

You have to take the time, dedication, and intentionality needed in order to focus.

CHARACTERISTIC ELEVEN

ENJOYMENT

> I think in life you should work on yourself until the day you die.
>
> —Serena Williams

As a teen, it can be so easy to get caught up in longing for the future. So many exciting things start to feel within reach once you hit the age of thirteen.

First, you head into freshman year of high school. Your awkward and excited little self has absolutely no clue what the next four years will hold, but you are just ready to get into the *real world*. Life is consumed by geometry tests and new friendships, and you finally get social media and data on your phone!

Fast forward, and you've got to start studying for your learner's permit. You worry, "will I fail?"

You pass!

Yeah, I missed a few questions, but who cares? I can drive now!

Age sixteen rolls around, and you pass your driver's test. You weren't perfect. Sure, you could have done better on that devilish parallel parking. But now you are legit.

You get your first paying job, and, unfortunately for you, taxes become more than a Boston Tea Party lesson in history class.

Guess what?

You are seventeen and an absolute dancing queen—or king.

Plus, your dad's old truck is now yours! You don't have to borrow the minivan anymore; you are free to ... well, free to pay for your own gas and pay for your food. But you are free!

It's something you can call yours!

Whoa.

Time flies, and you become a legal adult, age eighteen. You are older, graduating from high school. It's time to prepare for college. It's exciting yet scary.

Think about all you must get done. Scholarships, decorating your dorm, moving away from home, meeting new people, and starting intense classes.

Boom.

You are nineteen, in college and making a whole new life for yourself, and in twelve months, you will no longer be a teen.

Isn't it crazy? Wasn't it just yesterday you were taking your permit test?

Walking down the gray brick walls of your high school as a freshman?

Remember when you thought high school chemistry would be the end of you?

Or when you nearly forgot to submit that essay for English 101, so you quickly wrote it in fifty-one minutes *exactly*, submitting it at 11:58 p.m. right before the deadline, and you *nailed* it.

Time really does fly.

When you are thirteen, age eighteen seems like a million years away. It's crazy how one person can change so much between those ages, but we do. We face trials and hardships that shape us into the person we are today.

No matter your age, the teenage years are a special and important time in your life. If we are not careful, however, we can get focused on the soon-to-be instead of the now. The craziness of life can consume us, and we can long for the next stage.

Yes, the future is exciting, but we don't live in the future. We live in the present. The past can be full of regrets. But we don't live in the past. We live in the present.

Do you see your now as it is called?

A present.

A gift.

It's valuable.

There are always going to be bumps in the road no matter where you are in life. It is important to enjoy where you are and where you have come from.

If you do not, you will miss the little moments of life if you are always focused on the moments to come. No one actually can live in the past or the future. You only have now. You cannot change your past, but by living your best in the present, you can shape your future.

I am going to be transparent with you.

This is something that I still struggle with to this day. I have dreams and plans. I can get so focused on the future that I lose sight of my now. I can feel so discontented with where I am. I can feel my next approaching, but I am just not quite ready to be there yet.

Enjoyment comes when we embrace the now realizing that there is a season for everything.

There are things that I need to do and enjoy now that I can never get back later. I have to remind myself of how special this time is. Life is not always about work. It's about making memories, and if that means losing one night of studying to spend with my family, then that is what I will do.

Spend your time wisely and intentionally because time is money. You cannot get it back. Every second that ticks by is gone forever.

How are you using your now? Are you influencing your now, or is your now influencing you?

Taking the time to learn how to stop and enjoy the people, the scenery, and all the little things will be a weapon for you in the future.

Life is going to hit hard, but if you can learn to keep swinging no matter how hard you get hit, you will get so much further in life.

Even when it seems like the storms around you are causing chaos in your life, can you see the majestic power of the thunder as it roars or the beauty of the lightning striking the sky?

All things have good and evil.

Can you see the good in your world?

Even when you feel like you're drowning, can you see the light above?

Can you focus on the joy?

Are you able to see the *big deal* about the little things?

Remember, you cannot get these years back. Please, do not stress yourself out on perfection. No one is perfect. You do not need to get A's on every test. You do not have to live up to false expectations. Do not let life consume you.

Do your best and create time for fun. Of course, there is a balance that is needed between work and fun for you to make strides into your next. You can never be a teen again. Enjoy it. But enjoy it wisely. Find out what your passions are and find work that consists of enjoyment.

Not all work is fun, but can you see the worth and purpose in your actions?

I encourage you to work on a mental shift. Each day move closer to a positive mindset.

Why?

Our minds can easily focus on the negative. Negativity seems to be the default in life. You have to be intentional to embrace the positive.

Negative sells. It's what the news focuses on, tv shows, movie plots—negative is the way we are programmed to think. Anxiety is supposed to be the norm. *It is not.* Step out of the negative and see the joyous moments and things in your life.

How can you truly enjoy and honor the greatness in your future if you don't know what being at the bottom and still feeling content feels like?

If you cannot be content now, you will never be satisfied.

People will always want more money, more fame, and more recognition. But all those things are temporary and should not be your focus.

Your focus should be on the now.

Have you ever asked yourself how you can change someone's life so that they can change someone else's?

It is a domino effect. We need each other. We can't change the world by ourselves. However, You have a part to play. Maybe it is changing one thing. And through the help of others, then the world will be changed.

You have a story.

I have a story.

We all have a story and unique gifts that can help others. If you are so focused on the past or present, you will never be able to make a change in the now.

Stop saying you are going to start tomorrow because tomorrow will never arrive.

Today is the only day you have.

CHARACTERISTIC TWELVE

REFLECTION

> I love what I do. I take great pride in what I do. And I can't do something halfway, three-quarters, nine-tenths. If I'm going to do something, I go all the way.
>
> —Tom Cruise

Decision-making can be one of the most intimidating things we do in life because decisions have the power to change our lives. Decisions can be as simple as what's for lunch and as terrifying as deciding where to go to college or whether to end a relationship. Ultimately, our life is the result of the sum total of our choices.

Over the years, I have had to make numerous decisions as it relates to changing schools, who I hang out with, and what opportunities I will pursue. This process is intimidating, and adults tend to put a lot of pressure on us to know who we want to be when we don't even know who we are.

While you are in your teens, make wise decisions. Your decisions are going to shape your story.

I dare you not to stay in your comfort zone but to get to know people different from you, go places that are intimidating, and do activities that scare you.

You don't need to be like everyone else.

Who cares if you decide to play a sport for a year? It's just for a few months.

Maybe you do switch schools and realize your old school was actually a lot better than you thought. Go back, and embrace it as a learning experience that expands your perspective.

Most decisions are not the end all be all, but all decisions will impact and change you in one way or another.

One thing that has helped me process decisions and figure out who I am, who I was, and who I will become is the practice of reflection.

Reflecting can be done in many ways. You can do this by writing song lyrics, self-recordings, drawing, etc.

For me, I journal. Every morning or night, I reflect on what has happened that day. Sometimes I write pages worth of information; other times, it's just a short paragraph. But once I get my thoughts out of my head and onto something material, I can sort things out. I'll look back three days later and sometimes laugh at the thoughts that were bombarding my mind.

Most of the time, I realize I was overthinking, and it never ends up as bad as I speculate it will be.

The other thing about journaling is I can lay out all my options with the help of a "t-chart list," aka, the glorious pros and cons list. I make a lot of these, and they really help me see what I want, but then I have to create another column that asks how this leads me down the path He wants for me.

That's the hard part—trying to align my wants with God's plans.

Emotions can be overwhelming. Frustration can overtake me. But by reflecting, I can find clarity through all the thoughts in my head.

After you finish this book, I want you to reflect on who you were, are, and striving to be. To help you, I have listed questions below that will guide you as you journal: Now, if you are thinking, "I'll never use a journal, that's lame," like I said, you can reflect in whatever way is best for you, but make sure it's something that promotes action and brings you accountability. Something that you can look back on a year from now and see how much you've changed and grown as a person.

This tool, The Teenfluencer Reflection Assessment, will prompt important questions for you to consider. I want you to answer them honestly and without making it complicated.

This tool will help you find out where you are in your life currently, how your past has shaped you, and where you are heading on your current course.

Step into the action of discovering who you are so that you can unlock who you will become and be in the position to create an impact.

TEENFLUENCER REFLECTION ASSESSMENT™

- What are your dreams and aspirations? When did you discover these dreams? Who or what inspired them?
- What is stopping you from achieving these dreams?
- If you could change one thing in your life today, what would it be?
- What are you learning from the trials you are currently facing?
- What makes your message unique?
- How could your story impact someone else?
- What are your talents, interests, and gifts? How do these align with your dreams and aspirations?

- What is your next step when it comes to achieving your goals? What connections and tools do you need to create to get you to your next step?
- What is something you need to stop today that is holding you back from your future?
- Write a day in a life. What are you doing with your 24 hours every day? Are you using your time wisely?
- What is consuming your focus right now (TikTok, school, your job, a sport, an addiction, perfectionism, other people, your mirror, your next book, etc.)?
- Write down all the relationships in your life that have and are leaving an impact on you. Which ones are broken? Which need to end (they could already be out of your life, but are they controlling your mind)? Which should you invest more time into? Which relationships are filling you back up? Is there a relationship waiting for you to make the next move (a simple hello? A true apology, etc.)?
- What's been one of the most challenging moments in your life? And how did you overcome it? Have you really overcome it? Is there still bitterness hidden within you?
- What is your favorite thing about your life? Why?
- What do you do or think you need to start in order to keep yourself motivated and determined?
- What advice do you have for other teens? What advice would you give to a younger version of yourself? Is it the same advice? Why or why not?
- Do you see what you are invested in today as a detour, your profession, or a step toward your purpose? Why or why not?

PART 3

10 CASE STUDIES: WHAT TEENS CAN BECOME

Here is the thing. You can be number one in your field, number one in your passion, achieve all your dreams, and you will have a pretty good life.

Yet, your impact will be limited to your sphere of influence. You will not be able to change the world without the connections and help of others. Your name may go down in history, but that's what you'll become—history.

And at some point, the way history is communicated can be skewed or misrepresented. Information is lost, and significance disappears.

Think about the legendary artists from the 80s, merely thirty years ago. They don't have the same meaning to us as they do to our parents. We did not see them in person after camping hours outside the concert gates or wait years for their next album to drop. (Albums didn't even "drop" back them.) We can't appreciate their music like they did because those artists are in the past. Their moment has gone.

Some of us will have that moment where we will feel like we have reached the top. But you cannot stay on top forever.

Think about this when it comes to sports. A team can dominate for years, decades even, but at some point, they fall.

For example, the Lady Vols' Pat Summitt, the greatest basketball coach to live on this planet! Summit ended her career with a record of 1098–208 (.840) at Tennessee after the 2011–12 season, where she led the Lady Vols to their sixteenth SEC Tournament title and to the Elite Eight. She won eight National Championships!

Her legacy is *amazing*.

She paved the way for other coaches and the women's basketball league. I remember growing up and going to watch the Lady Vols play. I thought it was normal and expected for teams to score 100 plus points in a game because I never saw the Lady Vols not score that many points when Pat was coaching.

Unfortunately, her time ended too soon when she was diagnosed with Alzheimer's disease, and she had to retire, setting her records in stone. Now, with her absence, others have come along to surpass these accomplishments. When Pat died, the Lady Vols fell from their glory. Now, ten years since Pat retired, the Lady Vols are climbing their way back to the top ten.

This doesn't mean they won't make it back to championship level, but it does show that everyone has their time of dominance. One person can affect an entire program to the point where it's either success or failure without them.

Look inside you.

That person.

That person is wonderfully created and is destined for greatness. All of us have struggled with not understanding our why, searching for who we are, and finding our place in the world.

This might be the question of "who am I'?"

Why is this happening?

Why didn't this work out?

What could possibly be next?

Each of us has asked ourselves those questions. In the dark of the night, when we finally turn in and we are alone, left with just ourselves and God.

You must decide whether or not you want to pay the price to become part of the eight percent of people who achieve their goals in life.

It takes time.

It takes determination and passion.

The reality is that nobody can achieve your goals for you.

We've got to take off the fake smiles that our generation has created and put on the ones originally designed uniquely for us. We need, as the next generation, as teens, as dreamers, to stop tearing each other down. The level of greatness we can achieve alone is nowhere compared to the level of greatness we could achieve together. Imagine if every person reading this book invested first in themselves and then in one other person.

What would happen?

What if, instead of looking down on the next generation, we chose to raise them up? The effort of all of us together would exponentially increase the impact of our lives on the world. This is what I call the Teenfluencer Nation.

It would be a domino effect of change.

Can we shift the percentage rate of people who achieve their dreams?

Will we be the light in the darkness for all who come after us?

I believe in this generation that I represent.

I believe we can be the change. I believe in you!

We have the tools.

We have the people.

It is time.

If you are ready to step into or invest in the next generation, *rise up*. Stand up!

Take action. Walk by faith and promise yourself that right now, you are making the choice to be a light in the world. You are a unique light. Don't hide your brilliance. You are a flame that can ignite a blaze.

Let's start a fire that will spread from one person, from one location to another—a flame of perpetuity that will never go out.

We are the generation who will no longer be solely the influenced.

We will be influencers in this world.

We are Teenfluencers.

The world cannot be changed by one person. We are going to have to work together for the greater good.

When you look into the night sky, you aren't impressed by the darkness. It's the millions to billions of stars that leave an impression. There is room for all of us to shine, and together we will create a masterpiece.

You don't have to go far to find this Teenfluencer Nation that I speak of. You see it daily in every child and every teen.

You are here.

Welcome to Teenfluencer Nation.

Are you ready to see where we go, what we change, and who we impact?

Because today is the day we light the fire.

SIGHTINGS OF TEENFLUENCERS THROUGHOUT HISTORY

CASE STUDY ONE

RACHEL SCOTT
(AUGUST 5, 1981–APRIL 20, 1999)

> Don't let your character change color with your environment. Find out who you are and let it stay its true color.
>
> —Rachel Scott

A devoted Christian teenager, Rachel was unashamed to witness to others. Standing up for what she believed in caused her reputation to be hurt. People were jealous of her joy and the faith that she held. She was made an outcast and betrayed.

Rachel was killed for her faith by the Columbine High shooters Eric and Dylan. Rachel knew them before and understood they needed Jesus. The two were blinded by hate and, leading up to the shooting, had been bullying Rachel. They even made videotapes mocking her Christian faith.

On the day of the school shooting, Rachel was the first person to be shot on the school's campus. She was shot twice in the leg and once in the back.

After walking away, the boys returned seconds later after seeing that she was still alive. Grabbing her by the hair,

Dylan gritted his teeth and asked, "Do you still believe in your God?"

Rachel's unshaken response was, "You know I do."

Eric responded with, "Then go be with him," and shot her in the head.

Rachel's life shows the incredible ways God uses teens who love Him. Her life was only seventeen years long. Yet, God has taken her moment and turned it into a legacy. Her faith has touched millions through foundations and organizations. Her story is a flame that I hope ignites a spark in you.

You never know if this day will be your last. Are you prepared to stand up for what you believe even if death looked you in the face and mockery filled your ears?

CASE STUDY TWO

QUEEN ESTHER HADASSA OF PERSIA (400–500 BC)

If I perish, I perish.

—Queen Esther Hadassa of Persia

Fourteen-year-old Hadassah, who would go by Esther to hide her Jewish heritage, lived in Persia around 400 or 500 BC. When Esther was a teenager, the king of her land, Xerxes, declared all beautiful and virgin girls to be prepared for his presence. The King was to choose a new queen because his last wife had been killed (by his own orders) when she refused to portray herself in an ungodly way in front of the King's drunken friends.

Could you imagine what Esther thought as she was swept away from her family?

Now, to some girls, the idea of becoming the next queen would be thrilling.

Who cares what you have to do to achieve that title?

However, Esther was different from the other girls. The spark inside her made her shine brighter. Esther separated herself from the other girls who did not eat the way she did or believe in the God she did. Esther must have felt very, very alone.

When the King saw Esther, he was pleased and declared her the new queen. Could you imagine? It's almost like a modern-day Cinderella story. A young maiden of no royal position becomes the next queen of a powerful kingdom. The other girls, no doubt, would have been furious.

They were probably saying things like, "that loner was chosen?' The king will be bored with her. She was such a goody-goody! It's not fair!" Little did these girls know that Esther was only at the beginning of her story.

An evil man named Haman despised the Jews and wanted them all dead. He deceived the King into declaring that all the Jews had to be erased from the kingdom. Esther was told of this terrible plan and was instructed to confront the King about the situation.

The only problem is that no one was to go into the hall of the King without being summoned, or they would surely be killed.

Put yourself in Esther's shoes. You're the queen to a man who is about to unknowingly destroy the lives of your people. If you speak up, you will most likely die.

How would you respond?

Esther takes a deep breath, sets her eyes off into the distance, and determination sets in. Three days later, Esther approaches the King, and, to her relief, he lowers his scepter to her, granting her life, and offers her half of the entire kingdom.

She wisely declines the land and instead, makes a proposal. "If I have found favor with you, your majesty, and if it pleases you, grant me my life. This is my petition. And spare my people. This is my request." (Esther 7:3, NIV)

The King becomes outraged, not at Esther, but instead at the man who had declared this "vile thing."

And Esther turns to the hated man and says, "An adversary and enemy! This vile Haman." (Esther 7:6, NIV) The King then has Haman killed in a showcase way and gives Esther the power to write a decree for the Jews that she sees best, sealing it with the King's signet ring, which cannot be revoked.

Sometimes we are going to have to stand alone. We are going to have to speak out. And perhaps we will find ourselves in a situation where we have to risk our lives.

I challenge you to ask yourself, are you being timid at times when you should be brave?

Are you showing courage instead of bowing to the torments of fear?

Look at the life of Esther and ask yourself, are you destined for greatness?

Find the courage to take the next step and step up to your assignment.

CASE STUDY THREE

LOUIS BRAILLE
(JANUARY 4, 1809–JANUARY 6, 1852)

> Access to communication in the widest sense
> is access to knowledge.
>
> —Louis Braille

Louis Braille invented a system of reading and writing for the blind called The Braille Language at the age of fifteen years old. Braille had been blind since he was three years old and was inspired at a young age to create a concrete way to read and write. He took his burden and created hope for people struggling with the same condition.

Braille's language consists of a code of sixty-three characters. Each letter is made up of one to six raised dots arranged in a six-position matrix or cell. The dots are embarked upon paper and can be read by using one's fingers.

He later adapted the braille system to cover musical notation and published the first braille book, a three-volume history book, in 1837.

How can you take your struggle and turn it into an opportunity not just for yourself but for others as well?

CASE STUDY FOUR

MARY LOU RETTON
(JANUARY 24, 1968 –PRESENT)

> As simple as it sounds, we all must try to be the best person we can: by making the best choices, by making the most of the talents we've been given.
>
> —Mary Lou Retton

Mary Lou was the first female gymnast outside Eastern Europe to win an Olympic all-around gold medal.

After winning the US Nationals, and the US Olympic Trials at just sixteen years old in 1984, Retton had a knee operation right before the 1984 Summer Olympics in Los Angeles. She recovered barely in time and proceeded to win the all-around gold medal for the United States. This was only one of five medals she took home from those games. She was celebrated for her 1984 performance by being named the *Sports Illustrated* "Sportswoman of the Year."

How do you look at a setback?

Would you have the strength to recover from an injury and still compete to win your dream?

CASE STUDY FIVE

MICHAEL PHELPS
(JUNE 30, 1985–PRESENT)

> You can't put a limit on anything.
> The more you dream, the farther you get.
>
> —Michael Phelps

Michael Phelps won six Olympic gold medals before his twentieth birthday.

Just two weeks after his twentieth birthday, he claimed five more gold medals at the 2005 World Championships. He received praise from all corners of the sporting world.

Phelps would later go on to win six golds in Athens in 2004, eight golds in Beijing in 2008, and four golds in London in 2012. He has twenty-two Olympic medals overall and twenty-six gold World Championship medals.

Phelps has been celebrated as the World Swimmer of the Year according to Swimming World Magazine seven times, and was the Sports Illustrated "Sportsman of the Year" in 2008. He was named AP "Athlete of the Year" in both 2008 and 2012. Phelps holds thirty-nine world records and is the most decorated Olympian of all time.

Do you have the determination and willpower to never let anyone stop you from achieving your dreams because of your age?

Look inside. Strength awaits within you. Can you find the strength to raise your own bar?

CASE STUDY SIX

DWIGHT GOODEN
(NOVEMBER 16, 1964 –PRESENT)

> If you can get an out on one pitch, take it.
> Let the strikeouts come on the outstanding pitches.
> Winning is the big thing. If you throw a lot of pitches,
> before you know it, your arm is gone.
>
> —Dwight Gooden

Dwight Gooden began his baseball legacy career in 1984 at the age of nineteen, going 17–9 with a 2.60 ERA while leading the league with 276 strikeouts in 218 innings. He empowered Mets fans and tormented National League hitters with a fastball that caught fire at 98 MPH and a curveball that was known as Lord Charles. His 276 strikeouts led Gooden to break Herb Score's rookie record.

At the time, his 11.4 strikeouts per nine innings was the major league single-season record. Not to mention, Gooden became the youngest player in All-Star Game history. Plus, he won Rookie of the Year and finished second in Cy Young voting, even though his numbers across the board were better compared to the winner, Rick Sutcliffe.

Greatness is not dependent on a life lived long. Greatness can be achieved even at a young age. Don't let people despise your youth. You have greatness in you now. The world is waiting for you!

So what are you waiting on?

CASE STUDY SEVEN

MICHAEL JACKSON
(AUGUST 29, 1958–JUNE 25, 2009)

> The greatest education in the world is watching the masters at work.
>
> —Michael Jackson

Michael Jackson's father believed his sons had talent and molded them into a musical group in the early 1960s known as the Jackson 5.

Jackson joined the group when he was five years old and became the group's lead vocalist. He showed incredible range and depth for such a young performer, leaving a lasting impression on audiences with his ability to convey complex emotions.

Jackson and his brothers spent countless hours rehearsing and polishing their act, directed by a father who was verbally abusive and highly intense. Jackson, later in life, reflected on how he never had a childhood. He would stare out the car window on his way to the studio. Seeing a playground full of kids, wishing he could play like the normal kids. Yet he wasn't a normal kid. He had been working like an adult since he was five.

The Jackson 5's first album, *Diana Ross Presents The Jackson 5*, was released in December 1969, with its single, "I Want You Back," reaching No. 1 on the Billboard Hot 100 Chart shortly afterward. More chart-topping singles quickly followed, such as "ABC," "The Love You Save," and "I'll Be There."

At the age of thirteen, Jackson launched a solo career, making the charts in 1971 with "Got to Be There." He later went on to take over the music industry, and in 1982, his sixth solo album, *Thriller*, became the best-selling album in history, generating seven top ten hits. The album stayed on the charts for eighty weeks, holding the No. 1 spot for thirty-seven weeks. *Thriller* claimed twelve Grammy Award nominations and notched eight wins. Both of these feats were records.

Michael Jackson is the most awarded recording artist in the history of popular music and is recognized as the "Most Successful Entertainer of All Time" by Guinness World Records, selling an estimated 1 billion records around the world.

What do you do when your gift is not only your passion but your burden?

How do you stay true to yourself in a world full of the opinions of others?

CASE STUDY EIGHT

KING DAVID OF ISRAEL & JUDAH (1035–970 BC)

The Lord is on my side. What can man do?
— King David of Israel and Judah

King David was not born into royalty. He began life as a humble shepherd and yet ultimately built an unforgettable dynasty.

Saul, the first king of Israel, failed to claim victory against an enemy tribe, the Philistines. God sent the Prophet Samuel to Bethlehem and led him to David, a twelve-year-old boy who was a humble shepherd and talented musician. Saul was so impressed with David that he appointed him as his armor-bearer.

A major Philistine battle arose. The Philistines fielded a fearsome warrior: a giant named Goliath. Young David was not afraid. He had killed lions and bears before by the strength of God.

Armed with only a slingshot, he picked five stones from a riverbed and slung one at Goliath's head. David's aim was on point. The stone struck the giant and killed him. This one victory set David up for his destiny of being the next King of Israel, a very young King indeed, with great power.

Do you have the strength to face your largest giant and claim your dreams?

When you achieve your dreams and obtain power, do you have the strength to stay pure and kind-hearted?

CASE STUDY NINE

ANNE FRANK
(JUNE 12, 1929–FEBRUARY/MARCH 1945)

> How wonderful it is that nobody needs to wait a single moment before starting to improve the world.
>
> —Anne Frank

Thirteen-year-old Anne Frank wrote her experiences in a diary during the time of the Holocaust. Anne chronicled events happening around her which led to a vivid historical context based on her personal thoughts.

Anne often wrote about her feelings of isolation and loneliness. Anne matured quickly in her teenage years, and in her diary entries, her thoughts become deep and focused on her personal journey and humanity as a whole. She feels conflicted and does not understand why the Jews are being singled out and persecuted.

In her diary, which is comprised of two years of horrendous encounters, Anne deals with the complicated and difficult issues of growing up in the brutal reality of the Holocaust.

Anne's diary ends without comment on August 1, 1944, the end of a normal day.

Yet, her family, who courageously resisted the Nazis, was arrested on August 4, 1944. Her story comes to a silent end.

Anne's diary was recovered, and parts were published. Her simple act of writing told the unimaginable horror of the Holocaust and is one of the few accounts that describe those events from a young person's perspective.

Your voice matters.

No matter your age, your opinions, emotions, and thoughts can bring insight to something that is history in the making. You never know when your words will leave a lasting impact on someone's life.

CASE STUDY TEN

YOU (RIGHT NOW!)

Whether you think you can or think you can't, you're right.

—Henry Ford

Your story is being written. It is not over. You are merely at the beginning chapters. Don't just read it. Don't let others write it for you.

Live it. Be a Teenfluencer. Don't be a teen helplessly influenced by others.

Chapters will end and begin.

You have the power to throw in a plot twist here and there.

Other characters are going to come and go. But you won't. Not until the final page is turned. And after that?

Who knows where the pages of your story will find themselves and the impact they will leave.

We all have our own book, but we are in the same series known as *Teenfluencer Nation*.

The End.

A SPECIAL INVITATION FROM THE AUTHOR

I believe in you. I believe that you were created for greatness. I am looking for a select few Teenfluencers who are ready to become difference makers in our world. If that's you and you want to be considered to join my exclusive network of Teenfluencers, connect with me at kieracolson.com.

ABOUT THE AUTHOR

Kiera Colson, a senior in high school at the time of this writing, is passionate about sparking purpose and joy in the people around her. Through her writing, speaking, and coaching, Kiera is building connections and bringing opportunities for her generation and the ones to come. Born in Knoxville, Tennessee, Kiera grew up singing Rocky Top with her three siblings Makena, Aliyah, and Tegan. Connect with her at kieracolson.com.

SCAN HERE & LET'S CONNECT

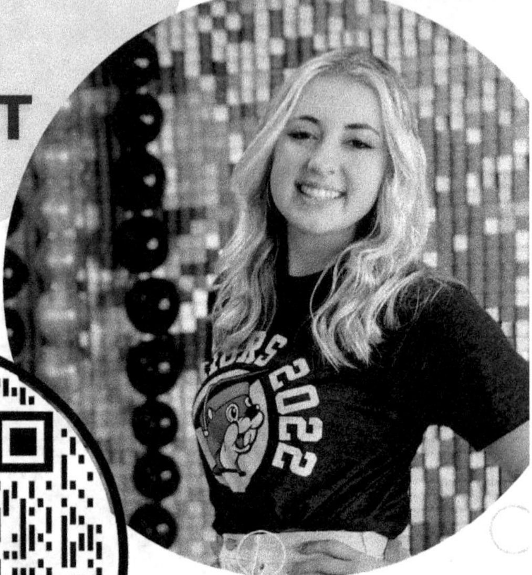

KIERACOLSON.COM

 @KIERA.COLSON
@TEENFLUENCERNATION

Check out the Teenfluencer Nation NFT

Earn Rewards

Complete Challenges

Exclusive Content

Discover Teenfluencer Nation Resources

Coaching

Bundles

Speaking Engagements

Courses

www.ingramcontent.com/pod-product-compliance
Lightning Source LLC
LaVergne TN
LVHW011939070526
838202LV00054B/4720